D0768971

WEIRD STUFF

Richard Tulloch

WEIRD STUFF

Illustrations by Shane Nagle

Walker & Company ❋ New York

To Agnes, Telma, and Bram

Text copyright © 2004 by Richard Tulloch
Illustrations copyright © 2004 by Shane Nagle

First published in the United States of America in 2006 by
Walker Publishing Company, Inc.
Distributed to the trade by Holtzbrinck Publishers

First published in Australia in 2004 by Random House Australia.

For information about permission to reproduce selections from
this book, write to Permissions, Walker & Company,
104 Fifth Avenue, New York, New York 10011.

Library of Congress Cataloging-in-Publication Data available upon request.

ISBN-10: 0-8027-8058-X
ISBN-13: 978-0-8027-8058-4

Internal book design by Jobi Murphy

Visit Walker & Company's Web site at www.walkeryoungreaders.com

Printed in the United States of America

10 9 8 7 6 5 4 3 2 1

All papers used by Walker & Company are natural, recyclable products made from
wood grown in well-managed forests. The manufacturing processes conform to the
environmental regulations of the country of origin.

acknowledgments *n.* ak-no-lej-ments. Thank yous to people without whose skill and help this book could have been a total, complete, unmitigated, undiluted, unalleviated, unimaginable disaster.

As Lancelot Cummins says, a lot of people have to help to make a book . . .

My thanks first to Margaret Wild, who saw some potential in a short story I wrote about Brian Hobble and suggested I try writing it as a novel. Thanks, too, to Sadie, Jane, Annette, and Rose, my agents at Cameron Creswell, for their support and encouragement and for doing all the boring contract stuff.

Thank you Eva Mills, Emma Royan-Smith, and the team at Random House, and thank you Melissa Balfour for your superb editing, picking up the mistakes, errors, inconsistencies, slip-ups, bloopers, goofs, tautologies, and the bits that were not so great when I first wrote them.

And finally, thanks to my dear family, Agnes, Telma, and Bram, and the many teachers and kids at schools I've visited, who listened to me read bits of this story and whose responses and suggestions helped me improve it.

R.T.

X-Rated information
(B.H. must have said it's ok
before you read this stuff)

WEIRD
STUFF

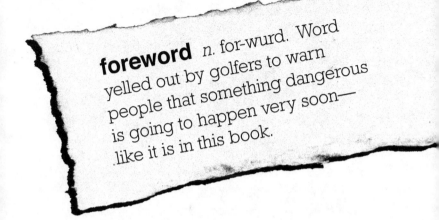

foreword n. for-wurd. Word yelled out by golfers to warn people that something dangerous is going to happen very soon—like it is in this book.

HI. I'm Brian Hobble: soccer superstar, boy genius, and red-hot babe magnet. I'm brave, intelligent, witty, popular, creative and, of course, fantastically good-looking—modest, too!

I'm also a writer, which is totally excellent because, as a writer, you can say wonderful things about yourself. You can say whatever you like about everybody else, too, so watch out! A writer is really bad to have as a worst enemy. In my book, I can make horrible things happen to people I hate. If I don't like a kid (are you reading this, Kelvin Moray?), I can make his desk open, slowly and creakily, and killer zombies crawl out and eat his eyeballs. If a teacher gives me a hard time, I can drop a bucket of cold puke on his head. (So keep looking up, Mr. Mackington!)

I wasn't always a writer. I had no imagination, or so I thought. But then this really weird stuff started

happening to me, and it was so totally amazing that I just had to put it down on paper. What happened was more than amazing. It was awesome, fantastic, unbelievable, incredible, extraordinary, unanticipated, and totally unportended. (In case you're wondering, there's a thick book called a thesaurus, which we writers use to look up all these long, impressive words.)

When you've read a bit of this story, you'll probably start thinking, "That Brian Hobble kid is nuts. That kid is a prawn short of the full chessboard. That Brian Hobble is a total Coco Pop!"

I want you to understand: I'm not some crazy mixed-up psycho. I'm just a normal, average kid (apart from being amazingly brave, brilliant, a babe magnet, etc., like I said before). I live in a normal, average family (apart from my stupid little brother, Matthew). I go to the most normal, average, totally boring Garunga District School, where nothing extraordinary is ever supposed to happen . . . and I don't believe in ghosts. As far as the supernatural is concerned, I'm a complete and utter septic—I think that's the right word. I'll look it up later.

So why did all this weird stuff happen to me?

stupefaction *n.* stu-pi-fak-shun. When someone people always thought was stupid does something good for a change and amazes everybody.

ZERO all. It was the semifinal of the district championships, so the whole school was watching. The game was nearly over. Our team, Garunga Glory, was playing our deadly enemies, Stanley Road State School. Stanley Road State was better than us. They were bigger. They were meaner. They had a coach called Syd. Syd had tattoos on his knuckles spelling *D-E-T-H* and a missing front tooth. Bad spelling, tattoos, and missing teeth are sure signs of a good soccer coach. Stanley Road had done all the attacking, but by some miracle they hadn't scored yet.

Stanley Road shots had slid past open goals and three kicks had gone over the crossbar. Twice they'd slammed the ball into the net only to have our linesman rule one of their forwards offside. (We had the scariest linesman on Planet Earth, by the way. She was our principal, Mrs. Davenport. Even Syd didn't dare argue with her.)

The rain had stopped now, but it was still freezing out on my left wing. The ball hadn't come my way for a long time. I'd only touched it twice all game.

4

That usually happened to me in soccer games. Nobody ever passed me the ball, except Vince Peretti. He was our captain and tried to get everyone involved in the game. He was my best friend, too.

Tattoo Syd must have told his players to press forward to get that goal they wanted. The midfielder who'd been marking me decided that if he wanted to get a kick he'd have to become a striker, so halfway through the second half he said "See ya, buddy," and trotted forward.

I jogged on the spot to keep warm, and stuck my icy hands into my armpits. I pushed my fists into my biceps to make the muscles stand out. (Did you know that's a useful trick to make yourself look tough when they're taking school sports photos?) But nobody was watching me out on my lonely sideline, so it was a wasted effort. It probably looked pathetic on my skinny arms anyway.

My chest was tightening up again, so I sneaked my asthma inhaler from my pocket. It wasn't the World Cup, so I wouldn't get banned for using a performance-enhancing drug. In any case, Mom had asked our coach, Mr. Quale, for special permission for me to inhale for medical purposes. Mr. Quale said that was fine by him, because my performance needed all the enhancing it could get. I took a quick puff and held my breath.

Then suddenly all this really *weird stuff* started happening . . .

The big Stanley Road striker sent a shot whizzing past our goalie, Sean Peters. There was nothing unusual about that. Even I could get shots past a goalie as hopeless as Sean Peters. The ball hit the post and bounced back into play. Our fullback Rocco Ferris swung his cleat wildly to kick it clear, and the ball came looping and bobbling out to me. I was on my own.

Please let me trap it, I thought. Missing the ball is not so bad when there's a whole jumble of players around you. You can pretend you were under pressure. Miss it when you're standing all on your own, and you look like a total idiot.

This time, my luck was good. The ball sploshed into a puddle in front of me, spraying me with muddy water. It stopped dead at my feet. I didn't look like a total idiot. I had the ball!

"Brian Hobble!" screamed the crowd.

"Kick a goal, Brian!" yelled my little brother, Matthew.

"Go, Brian Hobble!" yelled Mr. Quale. "You're the Man!"

There was nobody in front of me. I kicked the ball toward the opposite goal. It looked a long way off. About ten zillion miles off in the distance. I ran after the ball. My legs felt weak; really, really weak . . . how can I describe it?

There's a book called *Bone Suckers* about this disgusting boy who never changes his socks. These creatures breed in the cheesy gray stuff between his toes and then at night they suck the bones out of his limbs. My socks had been filthy at the start of the game, and I'd run through mud and even sweated a bit since then. Now it felt like an army of Bone Suckers had been at work on my legs.

I caught up with the ball, gave it another hopeful kick, and stumbled on. I didn't dare look back, but I could feel Stanley Road defenders rushing to cover me. I could hear their heavy breathing and Tattoo Syd, the coach, yelling, "Stop him! Get the little punk!" They were so close I could smell their BO.

I kicked the ball again. It wasn't real dribbling; I'm not skillful or fast enough to do that. If I tried to

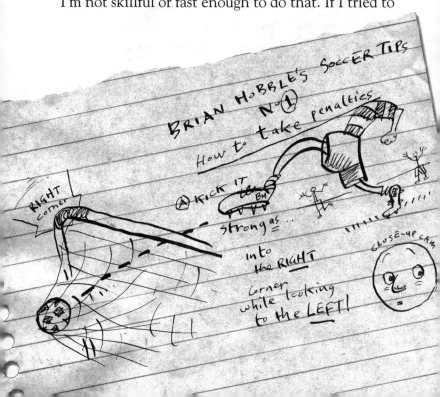

BRIAN HOBBLE'S SOCCER TIPS

N°① How to take penalties

ⓐ KICK IT strong as ...

into the RIGHT corner while looking to the LEFT!

RIGHT corner

BH

CLOSE-UP CAM

dribble Brazilian style, like Mr. Quale had shown us in training, they'd have caught me in three squillionths of a second. I hacked and chased, hacked and chased. I was over the center line. There was the penalty area ahead. I was nearly there . . . a goal would win it. One kick from Brian Hobble would win us the game! But would Brian Hobble ever make that kick?

I was too slow. Two defenders had caught me, one on either side. Six more steps and they'd swallow me up. We reached the muddy part at the top of the penalty area. I stretched out a jellyfish leg to give the ball one last despairing prod, and braced myself to get thumped into the ground. But then something *super totally freaky weird* happened . . .

The crunching tackle I was expecting from the Stanley Road defenders never came.

"I got him!" shouted one. At exactly the same moment the other one screamed, "He's mine!" From the corner of my eye I saw their feet tangle together and both came down in a heap behind me. The ball hit another puddle and slowed, so I could catch up with it again.

That still left a midfielder, racing across to cut me off. He was going at a million miles an hour. He'd get me for sure. I flinched out of the way, tapping the ball to the left.

The midfielder hit the mud patch and his cleats went out from under him. He slid feet first straight across my path, ending in a spray of muddy water and a stream of interesting language I don't have time to put into the story (especially now that it's getting exciting).

The goalie had to commit himself now. He left his line and rushed out to cover me. To my right I saw a flash of brown and yellow: a Garunga Glory shirt—support! Our center forward, Kelvin Moray, was running alongside me, arms wide, screaming at me, "*Brian*! Pass it to me. *Brian*, I'm free! Pass it Brian, I'm *free!*"

I knew I should pass it. We were in the penalty area. Kelvin just might score a goal. He's a better player than me. He's also a real ball hog. Kelvin Moray thinks he is so fantastic. He has never passed the ball to me in his entire life. No way was I passing to Kelvin Moray. I tapped the ball with my left toe, setting it up for a right-foot shot.

"*Brian, what are you doing?*" screamed Kelvin.

I shut my eyes. The goalie dived at me, slashing with his left leg, catching me on the knee—a stinging pain. My legs collapsed, the last bones sucked out of them. As I went down I saw the ball trickle toward the net, take a hop to the right, and slide past the post over the backline. I'd missed.

"Brian Hobble, you are a total idiot!" yelled Kelvin Moray. "Are you blind or just stupid? We could have got a goal! We could have won. *I was free!*"

The ref blew his whistle. The game was over. Stanley Road would go on to the district final on their better goal difference. We'd get the speech from Mr. Quale about how it was a good effort to get a draw, there was always next year, and how it was just bad luck that we didn't win this one. But deep down, everyone would know it was really my fault.

Then I looked at the sideline. Why was the Garunga crowd going wild? Why was Mr. Quale going totally ballistic, whirling his brown and yellow scarf around his head, dancing like some insane tribal warrior on a nest of fire ants? Why was he yelling, "Yes, yes, yes, yes, yes, yes, yes, yes, *yes!*" Because the ref's finger was pointing to the penalty spot—I'd gotten us a penalty. *We could still win!*

My best friend and captain, Vince Peretti, pulled

me to my feet and bashed me on the back over and over. "Great play, Brian! Awesome run."

Then something happened that was even more awesome, fantastic, unbelievable, incredible, extraordinary, unanticipated, and totally unportended. (Thank you again, big thick thesaurus book.)

Mr. Quale called out, "Brian Hobble, you take the penalty."

Me? I couldn't believe it. Mr. Quale had chosen me to take a penalty kick?

hypertension *n.* hi-per-ten-shun. The super stress you get when you have to do something you're pretty sure will go wrong and everyone will laugh at you.

KELVIN Moray couldn't believe it either. He dashed across the field to Mr. Quale. "Let me take the penalty, sir!" he pleaded.

"Brian earned the penalty, Kelvin," said Mr. Quale. "He can take it."

Kelvin wouldn't give up so easily. "Sir! I'm so much better at penalties than Brian, sir. You know I'm the best kicker on the team, sir."

"And you know I'm the coach," said Mr. Quale firmly. "Brian's taking it."

"But sir, Brian's hopeless, sir. Brian will miss for sure, sir." Thanks Kelvin, I thought. It's nice to know I have such great support from my teammates. You've really made me feel good now.

Kelvin poked a warning finger into my chest. "Don't miss, Brian!" he hissed. I wanted to poke him back, or better still thump a mighty fist into his ugly face, but I didn't dare. Kelvin Moray was bigger than me, and better at thumping. It might have encouraged Stanley Road to see the opposition penalty taker flattened by one of his own players at a moment like this.

Lucky for me, Mr. Quale stepped in. "That'll do," he said. "Let him get on with the job, Kelvin. Think of yourself as the Ice Man, Brian. You are cool in a crisis! You're cooler than a penguin in a freezer. I believe you can do this thing, Brian Hobble!"

Mr. Quale paced up and down, busy hands fiddling with his brown and yellow Garunga scarf, tucking it into the collar of his leather bomber jacket, then pulling it out again. His shoulders were tight and hunched as he scribbled in his notebook, then shoved his hands deep into his pockets. He'd coached Garunga District School soccer teams for fifteen years, but he'd never had a team that had made the district final. He knew how important this penalty was. So it was incredible that he'd picked me to take it.

The ref wiped the ball, flipped it around in his hands, and placed it on the penalty spot. Everybody was watching me: all the players on our team; the parents; Mom; my little brother, Matthew; and all the teachers. Mrs. Davenport was strangling her linesman's flag with a white-knuckled death grip. The kids in my class were all there: our cheering squad of Abby and Sarah and Sofie . . . and Cassandra.

Most of all, worst of all, best of all, Cassandra

Wyman would be watching me. Cassandra Wyman, the most beautiful, desirable girl in the entire history of the universe, would see me take the penalty kick that could put Garunga Glory into their first-ever district final. She'd see me become a hero. Or, if I screwed up, she'd see me become a total reject.

Mr. Quale called, "I believe in you, Brian Hobble! Believe in yourself. Be the Ice Man!"

I tried to look like the Ice Man, trotting confidently into the penalty area. It was a good thing nobody could see me on the inside—I was anything

but cool. Inside, something was churning away in my guts.

There's this book called *Brown Gunk from Mars*. It's about a boy whose friends dare him to eat this mysterious brown slime he finds in the bottom of his backpack. It turns out to be the spawn of little aliens who start building their dream home inside his body. My chest felt like those Martians were in there now. A small alien with a sledgehammer was trying to smash his way out through my ribs to extend his living room: *Thump-thump! Thump-thump! Thump-thump!*

Vince Peretti rushed over to me. "Your shoelace has come loose, Brian." I glanced down. My shoelace wasn't loose at all. Vince just wanted a chance to talk to me. He knelt in the wet grass and pretended to tie my lace. "Their goalie likes diving to the right on penalties," Vince whispered. "Kick it low and to his left, Brian."

Sean Peters sprinted across the field to join us. He was a useless goalie, but he loved being a part of team conferences. Sean hid his mouth behind his gloved hand so no Stanley Road player could hear his vitally important advice. I couldn't hear what he said either. It sounded like, "Eer olee allays ooves eft, Iron."

"What?" I asked. Sean took his hand away from his mouth and instead whispered spit into my ear. He said, "Their goalie always moves left, Brian."

"Thanks, Sean," I said.

"So kick it right, Brian."

"Thanks, Sean."

"And then he'll miss it, Brian."

"Go away, Sean."

"Okay." Sean went away.

"Left, Brian," said Vince. "Low and left." He clapped me on the shoulder and skipped back over the line of the penalty area. Sean touched his nose on the right side and winked. Vince flicked his head a little to the left and winked.

In the net, the Stanley Road goalie was clearing loose mud away from the goal line. Surely someone that big couldn't really be a middle school kid. He was huge, hairy, too, with heavy black eyebrows meeting in the middle. He shook out his arms to loosen them up. I swear his knuckles brushed the ground, even without him bending over. He stretched his arms sideways, finding the middle of the net. He could nearly touch both posts at the same time. He thumped both fists on his chest, psyching himself up. He reminded me of someone . . . I bent down and pulled up my socks.

"Bet you miss," growled the goalie.

"Your shoelace is undone, buddy," called another player. "Want me to get your mom to come and tie it for you?"

Other Stanley Roaders joined the chorus, urging on their goalie, "You can stop him, Kingo!"

"He's useless, Kingo!"

Kingo . . . now I knew who the goalie reminded me of . . . King Kong.

"Take him apart, Kingo!"

"Come on, guys," said the ref. "Play fair. A bit of quiet while the player's taking the penalty."

"Low and to his left, Brian," whispered Vince Peretti. Sean Peters stabbed his finger toward the right corner of the net.

On the sideline, Abby and Sarah and Sofie started up a chant. "Go, Go, Garunga! Go, Brian Hobble! Go, Go, Garunga! Go, Brian Hobble!" They danced around with their brown and yellow streamers until the whole school was chanting with them. "Go, Go, Garunga! Go, Brian Hobble! Go, Go, Garunga! Go, Brian Hobble!"

The Ice Man. That was what Mr. Quale had called me. The Ice Man, cool in a crisis. Vince Peretti and Kelvin Moray had better soccer skills. Big Arthur Neerlander could kick a soccer ball seventeen million times harder than I could. But Mr. Quale picked me. Taking a penalty was a mental thing, said Mr. Quale. You needed someone with a cool head who could perform under pressure, and today that was me . . . apparently.

Mr. Quale called out now, "Ice Man, you are cooler than a nudist at the North Pole!"

Well, if I fooled Mr. Quale, maybe I might fool King Kong in the net.

My heart was making so much noise that surely even King Kong could hear it. The alien renovator in my chest had tossed away his sledgehammer and was now ripping up old concrete with a pneumatic drill: *Tugga-tugga-tugga-tugga-tugga!*

I glanced over to the sideline. Mom's face looked strained as she gripped Matthew's shoulders. Matthew called, "Kick a goal, Brian!" I couldn't see Cassandra Wyman. Deep breath in, deep breath out. Low and left, I decided; kick it low and left.

The ref blew his whistle and the cheer squad shut up. Suddenly it was dead quiet. This was it. Deep breath in, deep breath out. The Ice Man. Go! Now, quick, before you freeze!

Three quick steps . . . at the second step my foot caught on a rough bit of grass. I stumbled slightly. From the corner of my eye I saw King Kong lean toward the left post. Oh no, he'd read it! Too late to change direction now; stick to the game plan. I stabbed my foot at the ball, not great contact. The ball skidded off the side of my cleat. It looped slowly toward the goal . . . to the right. King Kong was completely wrong-footed, but his arm stretched back. He reached the ball. He had it on his glove. He lost it again. The ball deflected . . . toward the right goalpost . . . and hit it . . . and bounced . . . *into the back of the net!* There was a moment of silence. Then the whistle blew again. The cheers— "Yeeeeeeessssss!"

BRIAN HOBBLE'S SOCCER TIPS
Nº ③
How to take penalties

"The DIRECT Shot"

Stress Markings...

Heart, kidney, etc...

Back bone bits

King Kong sank to his knees, his head in his hands. This was totally amazing! I'd never done anything great in a soccer game ever before. Now I'd earned us a penalty *and* kicked us into the district final. I was swamped.

Vince got to me first, tackled me, and brought me crashing to the ground. Bodies piled on top of me. I'm not a hundred percent sure but I think Mario Fenton kissed me on both cheeks. The weight of kids pressed Sean Peters's face into my ear. "Good one, Brian," he gushed. "I told you to go right, didn't I? That's what I said, wasn't it? Kick it right . . ."

"Thanks, Sean," I muttered. "You helped big time."

Muddy hands dragged me out from under the pile and carried me off the ground. They meant well, I know, but when you've got little guys like Vince Peretti and Sean Peters trying to hold you up by the legs, even I was too heavy for them. They dropped me into a puddle.

Mr. Quale shook my hand with both of his and ruffled my matted hair. "Nice cool head, Brian Hobble. Knew you were the guy for the job. The Ice Man in a crisis! Now come on, boys, a bit of sportsmanship. Garunga Glory, three cheers for Stanley Road, 'ray, 'ray, 'ray!"

We shook hands all around. The Stanley Road team had looked so ferocious during the game. Now they just looked like tired schoolkids with red faces and sweaty shirts. Even King Kong looked smaller as he pulled off his glove and took my hand. "Nice fake on that penalty, man. I thought you was gonna kick it low and left."

"Er, yeah," I said.

"Good luck in the final, man."

"Er, thanks, um, Kingo."

The Garunga girls swarmed all around us, Abby and Sarah and Sofie frantically waving their streamers in our faces. "Go, go Garunga! Go, go Garunga!"

I still couldn't see Cassandra.

Mom came over, holding Matthew's hand. Matthew's little moon face was shining. "You kicked it real soft, Brian," he said. "Was that a trick to fool the goalie? Was that your super special spinner kick?"

Mom said, "That was a really exciting win, dear. Were you nervous?"

Nervous? As if! Hey, I was the Ice Man now!

"Were you nervous, darling?" Mom repeated.

"No way."

I scanned the crowd behind her. Still no Cassandra. Where was she?

girl *n.* gurl. Young person of the female gender that makes you want to stand right next to her and run away from her at the same time.

I can't put it off any longer. It's time I told you a bit about Cassandra Wyman. I've said already that she was the most beautiful girl in the entire history of the universe, which might give you the impression that she was my girlfriend. She wasn't—unfortunately.

Cassandra Wyman had started as a new girl at our school at the beginning of the year, but somehow I hadn't noticed her until the last few weeks. Come to think of it, I hadn't noticed any girls at all for the last six or seven years.

I used to have a girlfriend . . . when I was five. She was Madeline Chubb, who lived next door to us. That was really incredible, knowing what Madeline is like now. (She's still in our class and, believe me, she is definitely not someone you would want as your girlfriend. She peers right into your face when she talks to you, and she's always eating Nutter Butter cookies. The smell of them sort of wafts in front of her like a toxic gas cloud.) I'm glad none of my friends know that Madeline Chubb and I were going together when we were five.

Madeline Chubb and I used to play hide-and-seek and tag in her backyard. We acted out little dramas, playing superheroes from shows on TV. She was Amazo Girl and I was Monster Muscle Man, and we zoomed up and down the street in capes made from Mom's dish towels.

Madeline Chubb invited me to her dollies' tea parties under the slide in the park. This is totally embarrassing when I look back on it; now I am the new, improved, awesomely mature, and totally cool me. But when I was little I used to go to Madeline Chubb's tea parties and eat Nutter Butter cookies. Worse, I used to take my toy monkey, Bubblegum, with me. Even worse than that, Madeline Chubb asked me to marry her. Worst of all, I said yes.

Fortunately, when I turned six I realized that Madeline Chubb was totally stupid, revolting, dis-gusting, abhorrent, repugnant, and abominable. (That thesaurus book was useful for that sentence, too.) I broke off our engagement immediately.

Madeline Chubb told all her friends she broke it off first. Okay, maybe she did, but I swear I dumped her three seconds later. So, I guess it was more like a mutually agreed upon separation. At exactly this time, all the girls in our class suddenly decided that boys had horrible habits and were dirty and had cooties and nasty body odors. Girls stopped inviting

GUIDE TO TALKING to GIRLS *

© B.Hubble

(A) RIGHT √√

(B) WRONG xx

Hey there BABE!

Err... Um... schlkblmm ... bah bah

(CLOSE-UP)

TONGUE-CAM

* Chose (A)

boys to dollies' tea parties, which was a very good thing. Because at exactly the same time all the boys agreed that every girl in the entire world was totally stupid, revolting, disgusting, abhorrent, etc. (see above for full list). Girls also had infectious diseases that we didn't want to catch.

So, on one side of the playground, juvenile girls played with their childish Barbies and discussed stupid teeny magazines and ridiculous pony clubs. And, on the other side of the playground, as far away from them as possible, we boys played really cool, mature, sensible, intelligent games with toy racing cars.

If, for any reason, a creature of the girl variety crossed the magic invisible line down the center of the playground, you had to put your finger down your throat and pretend to throw up. If you were unlucky enough to actually come into contact with a girl, you ran away wiping the skin she'd touched and yelling, "Ooh yuck, girl germs, girl germs!"

In the last few months, though, I'd changed my mind.

If Cassandra Wyman had girl germs, I secretly felt I wouldn't mind catching them. But so far she'd given no sign of wanting to share them with me. Of course, I wouldn't dream of ever letting any of my friends know I felt this way about her. I'd never live it down. I didn't want to come into the classroom one morning and see a big pink heart drawn on the blackboard with *Brian Hobble + Cassandra Wyman* scrawled across it. So I'd kept my feelings hidden. I'd been impressively cool. I was the Ice Man. No one could possibly suspect me of having any feelings for girls at all—especially not for Cassandra Wyman.

Most of the other girls had gone boy crazy. They painted their fingernails and drew little hearts in their notebooks. They giggled over secret notes they wrote to each other about who was in love with which movie star or who was going with who in our class.

Abby and Sarah and Sofie used markers to give each other fake tattoos with their boyfriends' names on them. This was really stupid, because every time they changed their boyfriends they had to change their tattoos.

DREAMS

April 12

I was inside a block of ICE
and no one could see it!

Abby Post had been Kelvin Moray's girlfriend up
until last week, but on Thursday he told her she was
dropped because now he was going with Sofie
Poulos. Sofie had been going with Arthur
Neerlander, but Arthur was Kelvin's friend so he
gave Sofie to Kelvin and took over Sarah Griggs
from Rocco Ferris. Rocco started going with Abby.
The next day Kelvin decided he wanted to get back
together with Abby again, so the three of them had
to shuffle around once more. This was especially a
problem for Abby, because after Kelvin dropped her

26

she'd given herself a tattoo that said *Rocco 4 ever*. And she'd done it with an indelible cloth marker.

Cassandra didn't get into any of that stuff. She was sort of quiet and serious. She never spoke much in class, but if the teachers asked her something she usually knew the answers. At lunchtime she normally disappeared into the library. She talked pleasantly enough to everybody who spoke to her, but as far as I knew she hadn't made any really close friends.

Up until now I'd always been too shy to speak to her. She never spoke to me. She was a bit cool. The Ice Girl. We were obviously made for each other.

After my brilliant success in the soccer game and the backslapping from my adoring fans, I was heading to the locker room to pick up my gear. There was Cassandra Wyman, coming down the steps from the main school building, slinging a heavy school backpack over her shoulder. She was heading my way. Our paths were going to cross. She was going to speak to me!

She sure was cute. Cassandra had to be the only girl in our school who could look good in the Garunga school uniform (yuck-yellow top and diarrhea-brown shorts or skirt).

Since I'd scored that goal, in my mind I'd been practicing the scene of my first real conversation with Cassandra Wyman. The encouraging part of my brain told me it would go something like this . . .

Me: (*super casual*) Hi, Cassandra.
(*Cassandra flicks back her blond ponytail and gives me a dazzling smile.*)

Cassandra: Brian!

Me: So, what did you think, Cassandra?

Cassandra: (*breathlessly*) Oh, Brian, you were so awesome!

Me: (*with a modest shrug*) Thanks, Cassandra.

Cassandra: I had no idea you were such a great player!

Me: (*with another shrug, even more modest than the last*) I've been practicing a lot.

Cassandra: I would have been so nervous taking that penalty, but you looked so confident, Brian! You just knew you were going to succeed.

Me: Cassandra, that's just the sort of guy I am.

Cassandra: (*clutching my hand and pressing it to her lips*) Oh, Brian, it would be just so fantastic if I could be your girlfriend!

Me: (*another one of those modest shrugs—I'm getting really good at them now*) Well, if you really want to, Cassandra . . .
(*Cassandra's eyes sparkle as she looks into mine.*)

Cassandra: Oh, I do, Brian, I do!

Me: All right then. (*Maybe one more shrug . . . or would that be overdoing it?*)

Unfortunately, this was just how it went in my imagination. The depressing part of my brain was telling me that in real life the conversation would be a totally awkward, embarrassing disaster. I was about to find out. She was right in front of me.

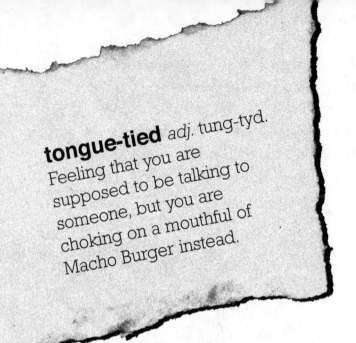

tongue-tied *adj.* tung-tyd. Feeling that you are supposed to be talking to someone, but you are choking on a mouthful of Macho Burger instead.

THE Martian builders in my chest were swinging the sledgehammers again: *Thump-thump! Thump-thump!*

What would Cassandra Wyman say about my goal? What would I say to her? I tried to remember that I was the Ice Man, cool as a nudist at the North Pole. Thinking that only made my teeth chatter.

I had two seconds to think of a clever opening line, maybe the kind of thing a great sports star would say to an adoring fan, e.g. "I suppose you'd like my autograph, honey." Not good. "Hey babe, you caught a real cool game, eh?" No, that wasn't the way to start either.

My voice went a bit squeaky. "H-hi, Cassandra," I said.

"Oh hello, Brian. How are you?" She flicked back her blond ponytail and gave me a dazzling smile.

Now we were back to the script. This was just how I'd imagined it. The Bone Suckers turned my legs to jelly and the Martians in my chest got busy with the jackhammers at the same time: *Chugga-chugga-chugga-chugga!*

"Um, (squeak) nice day, Cassandra," I said. You idiot, Brian Hobble. It's a totally disgusting day. It's been raining all afternoon and there's a freezing wind!

Cassandra looked up at the lead-gray sky. "Yes," she said doubtfully, "it might clear up later."

The soccer, Brian! Get her talking about the soccer match! "So-(squeak-wobble!)-o, wh-what did you think?" I asked.

"About what?" she replied.

This wasn't in the script. She was supposed to say, *"Oh, Brian, you were so awesome!"*

"What did you think about the game, the (squeak) semifinal?"

"The soccer?"

"Yes. The game we were just playing. Just now." (Duh! What other semifinal was there?)

Cassandra slung her bag across to the other shoulder. "The start was a bit boring, when nobody was scoring any goals." *Boring?* Did she say the game of the century was boring? Taking a penalty was a pushover compared to talking to a girl you really liked. This was getting tough.

My brain wanted my mouth to shut up, but my mouth was nervous. My mouth panicked and said, "Well, we had this strategy worked out, you see, to slow them down early in the game to take the sting out of their attack. Then Stanley Road applied a lot of pressure in the second half and Mr. Quale said we had to pack the defense and hope for a chance to attack them around the wings, but our backs played really well, don't you think? Even Sean Peters, who normally misses everything, stopped some pretty hard shots, don't you think, and Vince Peretti was unlucky not to score a couple of times . . . "

My brain said to my mouth, "You're talking far too much. You're going to blow this totally. Shut up and give the girl a chance to comment on your fantastic penalty goal."

Cassandra was looking past me, over my shoulder. She agreed with my brain. My mouth faltered to a halt, ending with another " . . . um . . . don't you think?"

I was getting a really bad, sinking feeling about this conversation. Maybe Cassandra Wyman wasn't so impressed with my goal after all. That's why she was avoiding talking about it. I'd fooled other people, but Cassandra Wyman knew that I'd blown the kick. She knew the ball only went in because I was lucky and the goalie dove the wrong way.

But before I could find out—

"Hey, Cassandra!" called Nathan Lumsdyke.

At that moment, of all the people on the face of

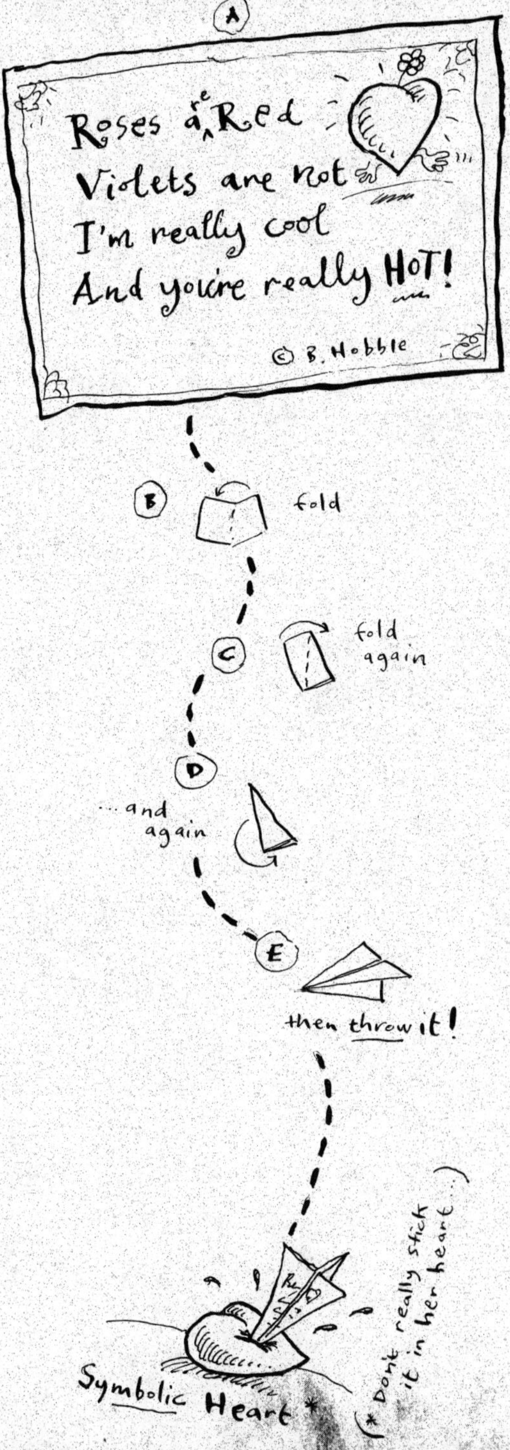
A
Roses are Red
Violets are Not
I'm really cool
And you're really HOT!
© B. Hobble
B
fold
C
fold again
D
...and again
E
then throw it!
Symbolic Heart*
(* Don't really stick it in her heart...)

the Earth, I least wanted to see Nathan Lumsdyke.

Nathan Lumsdyke was our class brain. He always put up his hand to answer every question. His assignments were always three times as long as everyone else's. We were pretty sure he lived in the school library. He'd read nearly every book in our middle school section and had permission to borrow from the high school shelves, too.

Now Nathan Lumsdyke was interrupting the longest conversation I'd ever had with the girl of my dreams.

Nathan slipped off his glasses. "Cassandra," he said, "I actually finished reading that Felicity Davids book, *Crisis in Creek Street*. I just returned it actually, so, if you want to borrow it before anyone else gets it, you'd actually better ask Ms. Kitto for it now."

"Oh thanks, Nathan," said Cassandra. "That's very sweet of you. I'll do that." She gave him a dazzling smile. The same smile she'd given me a moment before. Ouch!

"It was very informative, actually," Nathan went on. "It contained a lot of useful background facts about the Great Depression. Actually, I'd recommend it highly as research for our history project, if you want to get a good grade." He slipped his glasses back on and poked them up into position with his forefinger. "See you on Monday." Nathan headed off.

Cassandra shuffled awkwardly, too. "I should go,

too, Brian," she said. "I want to borrow that book Nathan suggested, so I can read it over the weekend."

I had to know. Deep breath in, deep breath out. Ask her now—go!

"What did you think of my goal, Cassandra?"

"What goal, Brian?"

"You weren't watching my goal?"

"Nathan said he'd help me with my history project, so we went up to the library. I found this great book by Emily May Debeen. Have you read it?" She pulled a book from her bag. On the cover was a worried looking girl in old-fashioned clothes, nursing a puppy with a pink bow on its head. Of course I hadn't read it. "It's set in the Great Depression in the 1930s. A girl called Molly and her puppy, Snuffles, move to the city where her dad's looking for work . . . "

This was disastrous!

"You didn't see the end of the game?" I repeated.

"Sorry, once I get caught up in reading, I don't notice the time. Who won?"

I couldn't believe it. The greatest victory in the history of our school and all the time Cassandra Wyman, the girl of my dreams, had been up in the library, reading about some stupid puppy called Snuffles! "We won one-nothing. I scored the goal from a penalty."

"Oh, that must have been pretty exciting, Brian."

Pretty exciting? It was more than pretty exciting. "We're in the district final next week. Garunga's never made the final before."

She shrugged. "I don't know much about soccer. No offense—I'm sure it's fun for people who play it—but to me it always seems sort of . . . dumb."

Dumb? Soccer was dumb? How could anybody, even a girl, think that?

"I guess I'm just not a very sporty kind of person. Bye." And she went.

There's a particularly fantastic book called *Escape from Planet Zog*. Captain Loopy fights off aliens with a can of Bug Zapper and gives his crew time to retreat to the Space Conveyor Ships. Then Captain Loopy rushes to the astroport, only to see his beautiful copilot, Lena Galaxa, take off for Earth in the last Conveyor, leaving him behind. "So now I'm on my own," mutters Captain Loopy.

As I watched Cassandra Wyman walk back up toward the library, I understood exactly how Captain Loopy must have felt.

GREAT MOMENTS IN Literature (as selected by B. HOBBLE)

"ESCAPE FROM PLANET ZOG"

By L. CUMMINS

(4 mi High)

Things were not working out as Captain LOOPY had planned...

mystagogue *n. mis-ta-gog.*
Someone who teaches you about mysterious things you never understood before, and you wonder why they're doing it, and whether they started all this weird stuff happening.

IF Friday afternoon was a bit out of the ordinary, on Monday my life became even weirder. On Monday morning, some giant hand turned my whole world upside down and shook it until parts started falling off.

First period of the day was English. Although English wasn't my favorite subject, at least Mr. Mackington made an effort to keep us entertained. Mr. Mackington could be strict when he needed to be, but he tried to make his classes fun.

He wrote on the board, *"JOKE OF THE DAY. Where would you live if an elephant sat on your house?"* Kids called out guesses.

"Sir, you'd live under the elephant!" called Mario Fenton.

"Nice try, Mr. Fenton, but wrong."

"You'd live under the elephant's butt!" called Kelvin Moray.

Typical. Kelvin Moray thought he was so cool and so funny, but he was a complete, awesomely stupid idiot. His friends were idiots, too. Rocco Ferris and Arthur Neerlander nearly wet themselves, laughing at Kelvin Moray's stupid joke.

"That will do," said Mr. Mackington. "If you've got a sensible guess, raise your hand."

Nathan Lumsdyke raised his hand. (Of course, Nathan Lumsdyke was always sensible.) "Actually, sir . . . "

Actually, Nathan Lumsdyke said *actually* every time he actually opened his mouth.

" . . . Actually, sir, it would be physically impossible for an elephant to sit on a house, sir, because it's actually an interesting fact that elephants can't jump."

"Actually, it's a joke, Nathan," said Mr. Mackington patiently. "If an elephant sat on your house, you would live . . . " he wrote on the board, "in a flat." We groaned.

After the feeble Joke of the Day, Mr. Mackington normally made us get out our books for a spelling test, which I always faled . . . sorry, *failed*. (Ha, ha, I knew that really.) But today, before Mr. Mackington could start the spelling test, there was a quiet knock at the classroom door. In came our librarian, Ms. Kitto, followed by a small balding man with glasses and a neat gray beard.

"Your Special Visitor is here, Mr. Mackington," she said.

"Ah, welcome!" said Mr. Mackington and shook the Special Visitor's hand. "I'm Douglas Mackington."

It always sounded odd to hear teachers use their first names. Especially when the name was "Douglas."

Douglas Mackington turned back to us. "It's our pleasure and privilege to have a guest with us today," he said. "He's going to be working at our school all week and, instead of doing our normal work, we're going to spend the morning doing some creative writing."

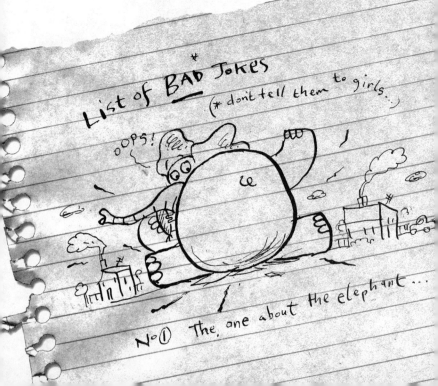

Oh, wasn't that just great? If I was bad at spelling tests, I was totally hopeless at creative writing.

It was a funny thing: Mom always said I could talk the leg off a blind donkey. I could think up fantastic excuses for being late for school. I could spin Mom great stories about why I had to keep old yogurt containers under my bed for six weeks. (I said it was a vital part of a top-secret NASA science experiment on mold growth in inhospitable environments.) But, when I had to write anything down, I suddenly couldn't think of anything to say.

A whole morning stuck in a classroom doing creative writing! It would be as bad as the time in *Escape from Planet Zog* when Captain Loopy gets held prisoner in a Zoggian jail, and has to spend all week cleaning out the toilet, the notorious Great Bog of Zog.

The little Special Visitor man polished his glasses and fiddled uncomfortably with his tie as Mr. Mackington went on with his introduction. "We're very lucky to have our guest with us this week. He was supposed to be teaching down the road at Marlborough College but they canceled due to a last-minute clash with their Gifted and Talented Camp.

"So, when his agent told us he was free, we grabbed him. We're pleased and honored to have him here. I have great pleasure in introducing our visiting author, Mr. Lancelot Cummins."

Lancelot Cummins? This little gray man was The

Great Lancelot Cummins! He was my favorite author.

Lancelot Cummins wrote *Escape from Planet Zog* and *Brown Gunk from Mars*, and piles of other great books like *The Ants' Pants* and *My Mom's a Zombie Killer*. I had them all at home. I'd read *A T-Rex Ate My Homework* seven times.

Ms. Kitto said, "I'll just leave you with Mr. Cummins, and I look forward to seeing the stories you come up with together. I'm sure you'll have an interesting time." She shuffled out and closed the door.

Ms. Kitto had to be the only person in the solar system who wasn't a fan of Lancelot Cummins. She'd stopped buying Lancelot Cummins books for the school library. When I complained about this last term, Ms. Kitto told me that:

(1) Lancelot Cummins books were the reading material of choice among criminal elements in the Garunga District School. His books were always disappearing from the shelves without being correctly checked out, never to be seen again. Furthermore . . .

(2) ninety-nine percent of the school population already had a complete collection of Lancelot Cummins books at home, and she didn't see why she should waste her limited library budget making Lancelot Cummins any richer, and . . .

(3) she didn't like books with farting in them.

Ms. Kitto didn't approve of his books, but Lancelot Cummins was famous! What was he doing here at Garunga District School? Mr. Mackington said, "I hope you'll show your best Garunga manners and give Mr. Cummins your fullest attention."

Of course I would give Mr. Cummins my fullest attention—he was my hero. He'd written *Brown Gunk from Mars*. He couldn't have been more famous if he'd been the world's greatest soccer player or the world's most glamorous supermodel.

We all clapped like crazy as Lancelot Cummins adjusted his glasses and gave a nervous little cough.

BRIAN HOBBLE'S Recommended Reading N°② *

MY MOM'S A ZOMBIE KILLER

L. Cummins

(* most of Lancelot Cummins' books are horrible!)

"Er, thank you boys and girls, and thank you, Douglas, er, Mr. Macker . . . ing . . . um, for inviting me to your school this week. I'm looking forward to working with you and talking to you and seeing some of your writing." He took off his glasses and wiped them with a handkerchief. Why was he so nervous?

"Um, you know, boys and girls, when I was a little boy, I never imagined myself becoming an author. I always thought that authors had extraordinary adventures and then went and wrote books about them. I thought authors were glamorous people."

I always thought authors were a bit more glamorous than Lancelot Cummins, too. He seemed very uncomfortable talking to us. His voice was soft and halting as he went on. "I was a rather shy boy at school. I wasn't good at sports. I was a . . . well, what you boys and girls probably call a 'nerd,' or is it a 'dweeb' these days? I never had any special adventures, so I thought I had nothing to write about. Maybe some of you feel the same way. Boys and girls . . . "

Calling us "boys and girls" sounded so childish. Authors who wrote great books like *My Mom's a Zombie Killer* should know big cool dudes like us hate being called "boys and girls."

" . . . Boys and girls," he continued, "everybody has stories to tell. Everybody's life is interesting. Everybody has experiences every day that can be great starting points for great writing. For instance, um, who had something interesting happen to them on the way to school today?"

There was a rather long embarrassed pause. Nobody wanted to be the first to put up their hand. I wanted to say something, just so I'd be able to tell my grandchildren I once spoke to Lancelot Cummins. I wanted to impress him by saying something interesting, or to make him laugh at a joke. But suddenly those aliens were thumping in my chest again. Besides, nothing had happened on my way to school.

"Come on, everyone," said Mr. Mackington, trying to help the situation along. "Surely someone stopped a bank robbery or got kidnapped by aliens?"

A few hands started to go up. Nathan Lumsdyke's hand was first, of course. "I actually had a very interesting trip to school this morning. I had my iPod on, and I actually was listening to a flute and harp concerto by Mozart . . . "

"Derrrrrrr!" went Kelvin Moray.

"Derrrrrrr!" went Rocco Ferris and Arthur Neerlander. They always copied whatever Kelvin did.

Vince Peretti caught my eye and stuck his finger down his throat, miming throwing up. Maybe Nathan had actually been listening to Mozart, but now he was actually showing off.

Lancelot Cummins said, "Well, thank you, um . . . anybody else?"

A few others began to tell their stories. Madeline Chubb had been barked at by a scary rottweiler. Jodi Helmson's little sister had thrown up in the back of the car. Other kids contributed boring adventures, like stepping in chewing gum or hearing the first cicada of the summer or missing the early bus.

Kelvin and his gang "Derrrred" every one of these pathetic ideas. As for me, my brain was in total blank shut-down mode. I certainly didn't want to give Kelvin Moray any excuse to say "Derrrrrrrr!" at me. Not with the whole class watching. Not in front of my favorite author.

Lancelot Cummins went on to tell us how he used real events from his childhood to create stories for his books. He used his imagination to turn the real things into odd, scary, bizarre adventures.

When he was a kid, three of his parrots died, and that inspired him to write *Pet Murderer*. Being afraid of the gurgling sound made by his toilet gave him the idea for *The Flushing*. Then he invited us to ask questions.

"Where do you get your ideas from?" asked Jodi Helmson. (Answer: "Anywhere and everywhere.")

"How many books have you written?" asked Sean Peters. (Answer: "Thirty-eight.")

"Do you have security guards following your limo when you go shopping?" asked Sofie Poulos. (Answer: "Ha ha ha . . . Oh, I'm sorry, was that a serious question? Well no, I don't have a limo and luckily I'm not rich enough to need a security guard!")

"How rich are you?" asked Kelvin Moray.

"Sensible questions, please," said Mr. Mackington.

But Lancelot Cummins said, "That's all right, I don't mind answering that one."

His answer was really quite interesting. I always thought that writers like Lancelot Cummins would be millionaires. But he told us that writers get paid only a little bit of money for each book that gets sold. There are all these other people who earn their living from helping make the book. There are the people who work in the bookstore, the people who design the cover and chapter headings, there's the publisher and editors, and they all have to be paid. So the author often only gets, say, a dollar a book. Not even enough to buy an ice cream, said Lancelot Cummins. That's why not many authors get rich.

But I was doing some math. What if a million kids like me bought *Brown Gunk from Mars*? If Lancelot Cummins got a dollar a book, he could buy a lot of ice cream. (Of course, after writing the gross stuff that happens in *Brown Gunk from Mars* he'd feel so ill he wouldn't want to eat them.) He would, in fact, be a millionaire. So what was a millionaire author like Lancelot Cummins doing here at Garunga District School?

There was another of those embarrassing pauses as he waited for the next question. Then Cassandra

WAYS I could get RICH
© B. HOBBLE

N° ① Rob ~~BANK~~ ~~Deli~~ my brother

Better use disguise just in case...

push finger (gun!) into his back...

Wyman put up her hand. "How could I become a writer?" she asked.

"That's easy," said Lancelot Cummins. "Do lots of writing. Do lots of reading. Have lots of fun."

Cassandra's hand was up again. "Do publishers ever accept stories from middle school students?"

Lancelot Cummins said that while there was no minimum age limit, larger publishers were sent thousands of manuscripts every year, so even many established authors had trouble getting stories made into books. It was unlikely that a young person would write something good enough to compete with professional writers, and he wouldn't want a young writer to get discouraged by the rejection . . .

His talk got a bit boring but Cassandra obviously really wanted to know what it was like being an author. She kept asking question after question about how many drafts he did, how he got started, who had inspired him as a child. She'd never talked so much in class before.

At last Mr. Mackington interrupted, "Well, lots of interesting questions there, Cassandra, but does anybody else have anything they want to ask Mr. Cummins?"

Another embarrassing pause. I scribbled a question on a scrap of paper and handed it to Vince Peretti. He read it and giggled.

"Ask him, Vince. I dare you," I whispered.

"Ask him yourself," he whispered back.

Mr. Mackington was watching us. He had ears like those aliens in *Escape from Planet Zog*, which could hear a whisper at a distance of seven miles. "Do you two have something to ask Mr. Cummins?" he said.

"Brian does," giggled Vince.

"Okay, Brian Hobble, let's hear it," said Mr. Mackington. I was trapped, like Captain Loopy when the Laserlight beam hits him just as he's climbing over the wall to escape the Great Bog of Zog.

Everyone was waiting for me to ask my question, and it was going to get me into big trouble.

I cleared my throat. "When you were a kid, did broccoli make you fart?" The class erupted. Even Kelvin Moray and Rocco and Arthur were laughing. We'd all read Lancelot Cummins's book *Escape from Planet Zog*, where Captain Loopy powers his spaceship back to Earth by eating broccoli, then lighting the gas from his own rear end.

Cassandra Wyman caught my eye. She was half smiling but, all the same, I wished I'd never asked the question. After all her serious intelligent questions, mine sounded really stupid.

Lancelot Cummins was laughing, too. He wasn't offended. Now that they knew he was hard to shock, other kids piled in with questions about the weird and wonderful things that happened in his books.

"Did you ever lose a gold nugget up your nose?"

"No, but my brother once went to the hospital with a pea stuck in his nostril."

"Was your big sister really a flesh-eating vampire?"

"No, but she did climb out the window at night and go looking for cute boys."

"Did your grandma really cook worm soup?"

"Ha ha, no, but her noodles looked a bit like worms." Lancelot Cummins seemed to be enjoying himself. I wanted to say something to show Cassandra Wyman that I did have some brains in my head. So I asked, "Are you going to write a book about this school?"

Lancelot Cummins said, "You know, sometimes

the most extraordinary ideas for stories come from the most ordinary of places . . . " (Well, you couldn't get a more ordinary place than Garunga District School.) " . . . but first I'd like to see some of your writing," said Lancelot Cummins. "Find yourself a pen and some paper."

This was the moment I'd been hoping to put off for a while longer. Just when we were getting on so well with Lancelot Cummins, he was going to see me make an idiot of myself. Because when it came to writing, I was useless.

FART Experiment (A)

By B. HOBBLE

WARNING (!)

Do not tr...

Really Rude section

RR Level 6 Security Req'd.

Lift Flap

trepidation *n.* tre-pi-day-shun.
Fear, terror, dread, horror, knowing
you're about to get in serious trouble.

"OFTEN I get my best ideas by thinking about things that scare me," said Lancelot Cummins. "What are you afraid of? I'd like you to write down something that you find scary. Don't think too much, just write."

Across the table, Nathan Lumsdyke started writing immediately but most kids looked lost for ideas. I stared at the blank page of my notebook. What was I scared of? Heaps of stuff I'd never told anyone about. The list was pretty long:

- Answering the phone when alone in the house
- Spiders (of course)
- Being swooped by birds
- Getting tetanus shots from the doctor
- The old lady with one arm who lives above the pharmacy
- I was certainly scared of talking to Cassandra Wyman!

No way was I going to write those things down. Because there was something else I was really afraid of. Something that scared me more than anything in the whole world . . . I was afraid of making a fool of myself.

It was all right to make a fool of yourself if you were Kelvin Moray. He was good at sports. He had friends who thought he was fantastic. He was popular. He was big. If anyone tried making fun of him, he'd just bash them.

You could make a fool of yourself if you were Nathan Lumsdyke. He was a nerd, but he could get top marks on every test. He could prove to himself that he was really brainy.

You could even make a fool of yourself if you were Madeline Chubb. She wasn't at all embarrassed about saying things that left her wide open for "der-rring." She'd just raised her hand and asked Mr. Mackington how to spell "boogeyman" so she could put it on her list. The Kelvin Moray gang "derrrred" her for that, of course, but she didn't seem to notice.

You couldn't afford to make a fool of yourself if you were me. I wasn't the best at sports; I wasn't the smartest at schoolwork. I hated to admit it (especially after what I said at the start of this story about me being so fantastic) but I wasn't even the best-looking kid in the whole class. And I wanted to be popular.

If I showed the slightest microscopic sign of weakness, everyone would make me miserable for the rest of my life. Then I'd never impress Cassandra Wyman. So I had to go into Ice Man mode. Taking that penalty had taught me a useful lesson. You don't have to be cool to impress people, you just have to look cool. If you don't say anything, don't show anything, don't do anything, then no one is going to say "Derrr!"

So what could I admit to being scared of? I scratched a couple of lines.

After two minutes, Lancelot Cummins said, "All right, pens down. Now, who'd like to read us what they've written?"

Up went Nathan Lumsdyke's hand, of course. "Sir! Sir! Mine's really excellent, sir, actually!"

Most of the time Mr. Mackington ignored Nathan Lumsdyke's hand waving, but Lancelot Cummins was pleased just to see a volunteer. "All right, we'll start with you . . . er . . . ?"

"Nathan Lumsdyke, sir." Nathan read in a slow, sing-song voice, with exaggerated expression:

> The yellow and red autumn leaves swirled wispily in the wind. They crunched crackingly under my feet and the sun set slowly in a blaze of glorious orange under a purple sky. I crept slowly along the drab gray concrete footpath toward the ghostly house with fearful shuffling steps, because I was scared stiff and full of fear.

"Derrrs!" from Kelvin, Rocco, and Arthur and groans from the rest of the class. I looked back at Vince Peretti, put my finger down my throat, and did that throwing-up mime.

Nathan Lumsdyke always wrote stuff like that. It went on forever but never got to the point. Someone must have told him once that to be a good writer you have to put in lots of flowery descriptive words. Nathan was really going overboard, trying to impress Lancelot Cummins with how brilliant he was. If he hoped to be congratulated on his genius, he was disappointed.

Lancelot Cummins just said, "Yes, thank you, Nathan. Some very nice, um, description there. Um, anybody else like to read what they've written?"

No more hands went up. Everybody tried to avoid catching Lancelot Cummins's eye as he looked around the room.

I accidentally on purpose dropped my pen so I could bend down behind the desk and get out of his line of sight. That way I could make absolutely, positively sure I wouldn't get picked.

Mr. Mackington picked me. "How about yours, Brian Hobble?" he said, "What's your spine-tingling story about?"

Everybody was looking at me. Cassandra Wyman was looking at me, which was a problem because of what I'd managed to scrawl on my paper. It looked bad when I wrote it. It sounded even worse when I

had to read it out to everyone. "I was scared taking the penalty at soccer—"

"Yeah, cause normally you always miss, Brian," murmured Kelvin.

"Kelvin, if you don't quiet down you'll be staying in to keep me company at lunchtime," said Mr. Mackington. "Start again, Brian."

"I was scared taking the penalty at soccer but I got it in. We won one-zero."

Lancelot Cummins said, "Well, er, that's a good start, er, Brian. I like the way you're starting to . . . express your feelings about soccer. Now maybe you could expand it a bit by telling us what made you so afraid taking that penalty. You know, 'I was scared taking the penalty at soccer because . . . ' and then tell us what it felt like when you faced that fear and overcame it."

I tried again. What could I put next? "I was scared taking the penalty at soccer because . . . because . . . " I scratched down a few more words.

Lancelot Cummins was walking around the room, looking over people's shoulders. He was coming to our table. I tried to put my arm around my work so he couldn't see it, but he gently moved it aside.

In *A T-Rex Ate My Homework*, a boy called Spike steals his teacher's lunch to feed his baby brontosaurus. When Miss Weevil finds she's lost her watercress sandwich, she towers above him. Spike's

How to Impress girls

By B. HOBBLE

No. ⑦

" Talk about stuff they like "

A.   flowers

B   Whales
     Dolphins or
     fish

C   The environment

D   Say you are against
     gender discrimination

was me all right. This time I did put up my hand. Vince put his hand up. Abby's and Sofie's and Sarah's hands went up together. Kelvin Moray's hand went up, and Rocco's and Arthur's hands dutifully followed their all-powerful leader. Soon there was a small forest of raised hands as the rest of the class joined in. Lancelot Cummins smiled at Mr. Mackington. He must have thought we were the most boring, unimaginative school he'd ever visited.

"Very well, hands down," he said. "It's time you heard the Lancelot Cummins Grand Theory of Creativity. You know, boys and girls, I believe that everybody in the world, and this includes people who say they aren't creative at all, has plenty of imagination." Huh, not me, I thought.

He went on to explain his Grand Theory of Creativity. It took a while, and I got lost a few times, but from what I remember it went like this . . .

If we didn't have imagination, we wouldn't get scared about bad things that were going to happen. If we didn't have imagination, we wouldn't get excited about good things that were going to happen. It took imagination to enjoy reading a book or even watching a film.

While we were reading or watching, we were using our imaginations to guess what was going to happen next, and that's what made it interesting for us. If the hero goes into a cave where we know a dragon is hiding, we get scared. In our minds we're

I was walking on the ceiling and all this gunk came out my ears

close-up

Dreams Nightmare March 7

writing the next page of the book, where the dragon eats the hero for breakfast.

"When I'm making up a new story," said Lancelot Cummins, "I'm trying to trick and surprise the people reading it. That's not hard to do, because readers will always try to guess how the story will end. So if everyone expects the dragon to eat the hero, I do something you'd least expect, like making the hero eat the dragon instead.

"We use our imaginations in daily life, too," he went on. "Suppose you'd done something wrong and you'd been sent to see the school principal. While you're waiting outside the door, how would you feel?"

"Scared," chorused a few people.

You sure would be scared waiting for our principal, I thought. There might be more terrifying principals somewhere in outer space but, on Planet Earth, Mrs. Davenport was the world record holder.

"Yes, you'd be scared," said Lancelot Cummins, "because in your head, you'd be writing the story of how the conversation with the principal would go. You'd be thinking up excuses, and trying to decide whether the principal would believe them.

"Writers aren't more imaginative than other people. We aren't more creative. Everybody has weird stories going around in their heads all the time."

It did make sense, the way Lancelot Cummins explained it. I did have odd stories in my head all the time. I could think up all sorts of revolting tortures for my little brother, Matthew, when he broke my stuff. That was easy to do. Unfortunately, just having ideas in your head didn't make you good at writing. When I had to write anything down, it always looked really dumb. I could never write more than three lines without getting stuck and not knowing what to put next.

Lancelot Cummins wrote on the board:

SETTING

"We'll start with something very easy. Good writers often set a story in a place they know well. Shut your eyes for a moment. Imagine yourself standing in the street where you live." I shut my eyes and thought about Brownville Road. It was just a street: houses, fences, driveways, power lines . . .

"Open your eyes," said Lancelot Cummins. "Now, see if you can write about what you would see happening in your street if you watched for fifteen minutes." He wrote on the board again:

FIFTEEN MINUTES
ON MY STREET

How could anybody write about that?

It was my bad luck to live in the most totally boring street in the entire solar system. Nothing ever happened on Brownville Road. People backed their cars out of driveways and went off to work. The guys from the development came every month to mow along the sides of the road. Our mailman rode along and stuffed the mail into people's mailboxes—nothing exciting. If I had to write about fifteen years on Brownville Road, I wouldn't be able to fill ten lines.

As I slowly copied the heading off the board

FIFTEEN MINUTES
ON MY STR ...

my pen stopped working. It probably had grit in the point from when I dropped it on the floor. I shook it. I blew into it. I sucked it, then stopped. Ink in my mouth—yuck! Shocking taste. Not a good look either, that blue tongue. I banged the pen on the desk.

"Come on, Brian Hobble, you've been given a task,"

snapped Mr. Mackington. "What's the problem?"

"My pen's busted, sir," I said.

"Actually, I could lend Brian a pen, sir," said Nathan Lumsdyke. Nathan Lumsdyke has the largest collection of pens in the entire hemisphere. He always has a whole range of different colored ones lined up across the breast pocket of his shirt.

"Thank you, Nathan," said Mr. Mackington. "I'm sure Brian Hobble would be delighted to borrow a pen from you."

Nathan passed a pen to me. It was a thick pink pen, marked along the side in flowery silver letters, "Easyflow." I pulled off the thick pink top and tried it out with a few creative scribbles on the back corner of my notebook. It had this pale purple ink. Yuck—this was the world's most disgusting pen. This was the sort of pen Madeline Chubb might think was cool. I couldn't write anything with this!

"Haven't you got any other pens I can lend?" I hissed at Nathan.

He'd already written half a page. Without looking up, he whispered back, "'Borrow,' Brian. I 'lend,' you 'borrow.' Actually, I don't know what you're complaining about. That is a perfectly good pen. It's one of my mother's special favorites, actually."

Great! I was supposed to write

FIFTEEN MINUTES ON OUR STREET

with Nathan Lumsdyke's mother's pink Easyflow pen!

I looked around the room. Most other kids were working away. Except for Vince Peretti, who had written two lines before running out of ideas and was now making spitballs under the desk. He was just as hopeless at writing as I was.

"Ahem!" said Mr. Mackington.

There's this character in *Escape from Planet Zog* called Andrew the Android. He can turn people into lumps of green plasma by staring into their eyes. Mr. Mackington was giving me that sort of Android

look now, so unless I wrote something quick I'd be turning into plasma in the next few seconds. I picked up the Easyflow pen and wrote:

*Fifteen Minutes on
Brownville Road,
by Brian Hobble.*

The Easyflow pen felt quite solid and comfortable. The pale purple ink flowed smoothly and swiftly across the paper. When I got to the bottom of the page, I noticed that my handwriting wasn't as scratchy as usual.

By the time Lancelot Cummins said, "Pens down," I'd filled four and a half pages with curly, flowery letters with little hooks under the *j*'s and *g*'s and flourishes above every *t*. I felt quite pleased with myself. My story looked really good. Then I thought of something else. Four and a half pages! I'd never written such a long story in my whole life.

Lancelot Cummins said, "I don't want to put anybody on the spot, but I wonder if someone would like to read us a little of what they've written?"

Nathan Lumsdyke's hand shot up, begging to be chosen. "Sir, sir, me, sir! Mine's actually reeeeeally excellent—pleeeease, sir!"

Lancelot Cummins was going to ask Nathan to read, but Mr. Mackington butted in and picked Vince Peretti. Vince was aiming a spitball at the back of Nathan's neck. Mr. Mackington was an experienced teacher. He knew who was about to start trouble. Vince slid reluctantly to his feet and mumbled:

FIFTEEN MINUTES ON
PLUNK STREET
by Vincent Peretti.

One day on Plunk Street an alien
spaceship landed. The aliens all got
out. The aliens all got out their laser
guns and the aliens blasted all the houses
and they blasted all the trees and they
blasted all the street lamps and they
blasted all the people and all the fences
and all the flowers and all the babies.
Then after fifteen minutes, the
aliens flew away.

He sat down. Lancelot Cummins tried to be encouraging. "Thank you, er, good," he said. "Lots of, um, action."

"Is that all you wrote?" asked Mr. Mackington.

"Nothing would have happened after that, sir," said Vince, "'cause the aliens had blasted everything."

I couldn't resist laughing a bit. I tried to hide the laugh behind my hand and it came out as this humongous snort, like a Zoggian fart but without the stink. Snorting is a bad thing to do in class because the teacher notices you.

"Ah, you're still with us, Brian Hobble!" said Mr. Mackington. "Let's hear yours."

I stood in my place and tried to focus on the purple writing, which flipped and curled and danced across the page. My throat was as dry as Captain Loopy's in *Escape from Planet Zog* when the alien army attacked just as the hyper-drive lever broke off in his hand.

I had suddenly realized something very odd. I couldn't remember anything at all about the story I'd written. Four and a half pages and I couldn't remember writing a single word. So I began to read:

*Fifteen Minutes on
Brownville Road,
by Brian Hobble.*

Arabella's delicate hand parted the lace curtains of her Brownville Road apartment. Her heart was pounding beneath the thin cotton of her blouse. Surely Trent would come soon. Already it seemed like a year since she had felt his hot breath on her neck, his rough mailman's fingers entwining themselves in her thick auburn hair. Yet it had only been yesterday that she had kissed . . .

Kids who had been staring blankly out the window turned to stare at me instead. "Derr . . . !" came Kelvin Moray's voice. Arthur Neerlander said, "Shut up, Kelvin. I want to hear this."

"So do I," said Lancelot Cummins firmly. There was no escape. I had to read on . . .

Then suddenly there was Trent, hurtling round the corner and bouncing down Brownville Road, his bicycle leaping the gutters like a knight's black stallion, his strong forearms pulling it to a halt right by her mailbox. How handsome he looks in his uniform, thought Arabella. Joy welled in Arabella's breast as she threw open the front door and ran down the path to meet him. Strangling a little cry of pleasure, she flung herself into Trent's hot embrace, and smothered his face with . . . passionate kisses . . .

I couldn't remember writing any of this! My voice faded to a whisper. "Don't stop now, Brian," said Mr. Mackington. "This is just getting interesting."

At first I had to force myself to carry on. Then, the more I read, the more I wanted to know how this gripping tale would end. It went for four and a half pages—an amazing, rip-roaring love story about a handsome mailman called Trent and a beautiful lonely woman called Arabella. It was full of beads of sweat on heaving bosoms and hairy chests. It had kissing in every second sentence.

My story ended with a tragedy. A fierce storm sent a tidal wave flooding down Brownville Road. Trent saved Arabella's life but, with a final ring of his mailman's bicycle bell, he was swept to his death down a storm drain. The more I read, the more I got into it. I was all choked up as the story finished.

I tore my eyes away from the flowery purple writing. I looked around the class. Kelvin Moray was too surprised to say "Derrrr." Madeline Chubb was crying. Vince Peretti's face was turning purple and he was biting the back of his hand. His whole body was shaking, like the time he bet me he could fit a whole Macho Burger in his mouth and nearly choked to death. Only he wasn't choking this time: he was trying not to laugh. Cassandra Wyman was staring at me. The bell rang for recess.

GREAT MOMENTS IN Literature
(as selected by B. HOBBLE)

"BROWN GUNK from Mars"
(By L. cummins)

This is no ordinary after lunch tummy rumble, thought Nigel.

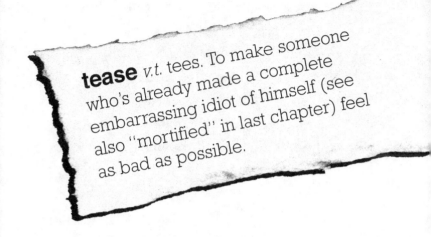

tease *v.t.* tees. To make someone who's already made a complete embarrassing idiot of himself (see also "mortified" in last chapter) feel as bad as possible.

I knew there was going to be trouble. Kids couldn't write stories like I'd just written without causing a huge reaction. If you write a story like that Arabella stuff, you get made fun of for the rest of your life. And that's just by your friends. Your enemies really twist the knife into you.

At recess, Abby Post came up to me with Sarah Griggs and Sofie Poulos. Those three always did everything together, as if they were joined together like the Siamese triplets who share a brain in Lancelot Cummins's book *Three's a Crowd*. Except that in my opinion, Abby and Sarah and Sofie didn't have a brain to share among them. Maybe they shared a lump of foam rubber that filled the gaps between their ears.

"Your story was so beautiful, Brian," said Abby.

"I never knew the Ice Man was such a sensitive new-age guy."

"It was gorgeous, Brian," said Sarah.

"Just so really . . . gorgeous!" added Sofie.

It took me a while to realize they were serious. They liked my story and they liked me for writing it. This didn't feel too bad, having girls drooling all over me, thinking I was wonderful. It was a new experience, even if it was only Abby and Sarah and Sofie. The trouble was that coming across the playground, hearing every word, were Kelvin, Rocco, and Arthur.

Kelvin Moray didn't like other people getting attention from his girlfriend, Abby (or was Sarah his girlfriend today?). He and his friends were going to give me a really hard time. Kelvin Moray fluttered his eyelashes and clasped his hands under his chin. "Oh, Ice Man, you are sooooo sensitive! You are sooo talented at writing. I think I love you! I want to marry you. I want to have your babies!"

"You wrote such a beoootiful story, Brian!" said Rocco Ferris. They rolled about laughing and I felt my face reddening. I was never going to live this down.

Now that they saw their boyfriends making fun of me, Abby and Sarah and Sofie had to join in the Make Brian Hobble Feel Bad party. They had to pretend they thought I was a stupid show-off for writing stuff like that. Abby said, "Ooooh, you are such a great writer, Brian, I want to marry you!"

"Pleeeease can we get engaged, Ice Man?" said Sarah.

I stepped away, trying to ignore them. Behind me, Arthur Neerlander called, "Kissy kissy wissy!"

All over the playground, little groups of kids were huddled together. They were all laughing and giggling. Every now and then someone would look up and point at me. I imagined they were all talking about me. In ten minutes it would be all around the school. I would no longer be Brian Hobble, the Ice Man; Brian Hobble, the soccer hero. I'd be Brian Hobble, the wussy kid who wrote stories with kissing in them.

Fortunately, I still had one friend left—Vince Peretti.

"Awesome stunt, Brian Hobble!" he said when he caught up with me. "You shoulda seen old Macka's face when you were reading that kissing stuff. Lancelot Cummins was impressed, too. And you got Madeline Chubb blubbing—what a beauty!"

"Yeah, Vince. Er, good trick, wasn't it?" I said.

"Awesome story, Brian! Where'd you copy it from?"

I was saved! Vince Peretti was my best friend,

and he'd come up with the perfect solution to my problem. Of course! I could say I copied the story.

"Where'd you copy the story from, Brian?" Vince repeated.

"Oh, just some book I read."

"A book with kissing in it?"

"No, no, no," I said quickly.

"But you said . . . "

"I just read parts of it, Vince."

"The kissing parts."

"Er, yeah. Pretty funny, weren't they?"

"Awesome, Brian."

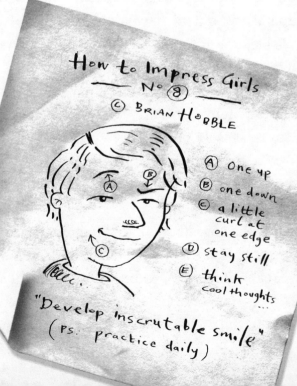

Unfortunately, Vince still wasn't satisfied. "I wouldn't mind seeing that kissing book," he said.

"Well, you can't, Vince."

"Have you got it in the classroom, Brian?"

"No."

"So you didn't copy the story; you knew it by heart! Awesome!" said Vince. He thought for a moment, then asked, "How come you memorized a whole kissing book?"

In Lancelot Cummins's book *Ninjas in the Bathtub*, the Evil Warlord Kragi always smiles an inscrutable smile so nobody can tell what he's thinking. I tried for weeks to develop a smile like that, watching myself in the bathroom mirror. I plastered one eyebrow down with invisible tape and practiced arching the other eyebrow on its own. Then I'd curl the left corner of my mouth just slightly. It looked really inscrutable to me.

Now was my chance to test out skills I'd developed under match conditions. I arched one eyebrow and curled my lip into the most inscrutable smile I'd ever done in my life. I turned my back on Vince and strolled casually over to get a drink at the water fountain. Evil Warlord Kragi would have been proud of my performance.

Then I noticed I had the pink Easyflow pen stuck in the breast pocket of my shirt. Where had that love story come from? I couldn't believe it had just come out of my head.

In Lancelot Cummins's book *The Flushing*, a psychiatrist treats Zeke for his toiletophobia. (That's a rare mental illness that makes people afraid to flush toilets.) The psychiatrist, Dr. Brainscrambler, tells Zeke that everyone has weird ideas from their earlier life floating around in their heads. He hypnotizes Zeke and takes him deep

BRIAN HOBBLE'S
RECommended
BOOKS

THE
flushing
By Lance Cummins

RATING ¹¹/₁₀ !!
✓✓✓

into his subconscious imagination, so he can remember being a little boy.

Zeke is soon sucking his thumb and crying for his mommy. Dr. Brainscrambler takes Zeke back to the tragic day when he's five years old and his cruel sister tortures him by flushing his pet goldfish away. That traumatic experience explains why Zeke is so scared of flushing toilets. Dr. Brainscrambler explains that he can't get anything out of Zeke's mind that he didn't already have in there.

If Dr. Brainscrambler had it right, I must have had that tearjerker wafting around in my brain all the time. Maybe I'd seen it on daytime TV, or read it in a magazine in a dentist's waiting room. Maybe I'd forgotten about the story but all it needed was a trigger to make it come out. A trigger, like the excitement of scoring my goal, or talking to Cassandra Wyman, or meeting my favorite author, Lance Cummins . . . or borrowing a pink pen with pale purple ink.

One thing was for sure. I'd never written anything like that until I'd borrowed Nathan Lumsdyke's Easyflow pen. But a pen couldn't write stories all by itself. The purple writing was certainly more flowery and neater than my usual scribble, but it was still my handwriting. *It was totally weird.*

I could solve this problem any time I liked. I could throw away the pen and pretend I'd lost it. I could give it back to Nathan and go back to being my old unimaginative self. But if I did that I'd spend the rest of my life wondering what had happened.

The bell rang to call us back into class. I could feel someone's eyes boring into my back like a Zoggian Laserlight beam. I turned around. Cassandra Wyman was watching me. Our eyes met. For a moment I thought she was going to look away and pretend she hadn't seen me. Then she gave me one of those dazzling smiles.

I decided to give the Easyflow pen another try.

vivisection n. vi-vid-sek-shun. Cutting the body of a small animal into colorful sections for scientific research, educational purposes, or fun.

AFTER recess we had science with Ms. Frankton. Perfect! In science there wasn't any room for imagination. I'd be able to see who was really in control, the Easyflow pen or me. Science was all about cold hard facts. Not that Ms. Frankton was cold and hard. She liked to be a colorful personality who could have been teaching drama rather than science.

"Top of the morning to you all, my darling little Einsteins and Marie Curies," trilled Ms. Frankton in her singsongy voice. "What a delight it is to see your eager young faces turned my way, thirsting for the knowledge it is my privilege to impart. Don't-fiddle-with-that-gas-tap-Arthur-Neerlander-You'll-destroy-the-whole-class-in-a-tragic-explosion-and-what-will-I-tell-your-parents?"

Ms. Frankton was strange. Perhaps she'd been exposed to too many chemical fumes in the science lab.

"I hope you little darlings found time, in your busy weekend schedule of TV watching and video-game playing, to do a little studying. Because, my dear little piranhas, you may recall that today we are having a test!" She shuffled around the room, handing out test papers.

"The past few weeks we have had a fascinating time, becoming educated about the lifestyle and

WHAt HAppeneD to Ms. Frankton to make her strange

(This does not mean she smells nice)

Hole where Mr. Red pants sucked out her Soul

I want my Soul back... mister Redpants!

Ms. Frankton

physiology of the frog. Put-the-top-back-on-that-jar-Kelvin-Moray-It-smells-funny-because-it's-sulphuric-acid-and-if-I-make-you-drink-it-you'll-find-out-just-how-funny-it-is! Thank you, that's better. Now today we are going to have a little test. Today we are about to discover what you remember about our study of our fascinating amphibian friends."

Our study of frogs had been the most memorable work we'd ever done in science. I could remember heaps about it. I remembered using tea strainers and peanut butter jars to catch tadpoles in the muddy pond down in the Urban Forest Area. I remembered Madeline Chubb falling in. I remembered our classroom tadpoles swimming around Ms. Frankton's fish tank, then growing their first legs and arms. Who could forget coming into the science lab, the morning after the long weekend, to find dozens of fat little frogs hopping all over the floor? Who could forget, too, the soft squishy sound as Sarah Griggs stepped on one? Sofie Poulos wouldn't forget Rocco Ferris putting a frog down the back of her neck either.

Ms. Frankton had finished handing out the papers now.

"You have precisely thirty minutes to commit the sum total of your knowledge of frogs to paper.

One measly little half hour to complete this science test . . . "

The most memorable lesson of the past weeks was when we had to divide into groups and dissect a frog with a scalpel. The smell of the formalin as we opened the glass jar would stay with me forever. So would the argument about who was brave enough to stick their fingers into the jar and extract the little frog corpse.

I remembered the first cut, the scalpel slicing into the frog's soft slimy belly . . . the guts spilling out . . . that moment when Jody Helmson threw up . . . into the hood of Sean Peters's parka!

Ms. Frankton had been very understanding, as I well remembered. "Settle down, everyone," she said. "Jody couldn't help it. Lots of great scientists had weak stomachs when they were young. Kelvin-Moray-you-are-staying-in-at-lunchtime-It's-not-at-all-funny-to-pull-that-hood-over-Sean-Peters's-head!"

Somehow though, I didn't think those Great Moments in Science would be part of Ms. Frankton's test.

"The eagerly awaited moment of truth has arrived!" she announced now. "You may turn your papers over and commence writing! *Bonne chance!*"

Well, this was it! I had the perfect opportunity to try out the Easyflow pen under safety-controlled conditions. In a science test there was no chance of the pen writing about lovesick mailmen kissing lonely housewives.

Question One, I read. *In your own words, describe the life cycle of the frog.* The life cycle of the frog? Eggs, tadpoles, legs . . . Great, I knew the answer! I took out the Easyflow pen. I saw my hand was shaking. It wasn't too late to pull out. I could pretend my pen wasn't working and ask Ms. Frankton to lend me a pencil. I could slip the Easyflow pen back to Nathan Lumsdyke right now . . .

But I was curious. This was science, after all. We were supposed to be doing experiments. The whole idea of science was to try things out and discover the truth. I pulled the pink cap off the pen. I began writing . . .

It seemed as if the pen had just touched the paper when Ms. Frankton's voice rapped out, "Pens down now! Coming, ready or not! Your time has expired, run up the curtain, and gone to meet its maker. This is an ex-test!"

What was going on? The test had just started, so why was she stopping us from writing?

I looked around the room, but nobody else seemed to be surprised. They were all putting down their pens, leaning back in their desks, sighing with the relief of having one more science test out of the way. I looked at my watch. Eleven forty-five. Exactly half an hour had passed since the test began. I didn't remember a thing about that time. I felt like Professor Pinquiddick in *Escape from Planet Zog*, who gets beamed up by the Zoggians and deposited back on Earth with his memory bank wiped clean.

But on the desk in front of me was proof that I hadn't been beamed anywhere. I'd spent the last half hour completing my science test, and there it was, all finished, in curly purple writing, with the Easyflow pen neatly placed beside it.

I'd written a six-page answer to Question One!

The carolling song of magpies echoed across the playground as Miranda crouched, naked and alone, behind the Bunsen burners on the science lab shelf. How she longed to be back in Ms. Frankton's fish tank, swimming next to Giles again, feeling his smooth dark skin next to hers. If only Giles had grown legs at the same time as she had . . .

The pen had turned my answer into a love story about two tadpoles from our science lessons. It was incredible. It was incredibly scary. I couldn't remember writing anything. I was like Professor Pinquiddick when he discovers that he's lost a whole year and that he's spent the missing time as a spy for the Zoggians, photocopying secret plans of Captain Loopy's spaceship.

Ms. Frankton was collecting up the test papers. I quickly read on . . .

. . . A bell rang, urgently. The door burst open, flooding sunlight across the classroom floor, and Miranda saw that she was not alone. Frogs like her were hopping everywhere, desperately dodging the feet of the stamping, squealing giants who invaded. Miranda watched in horror as one last frog hopped from the fish tank and flopped to the ground.

"Giles!" she called, "Oh my dear, darling, Giles! You are in deadly danger! Save yourself!" But it was too late. Miranda

I'd written the whole history of the frogs in our lab, but I'd written it from a frog's point of view—as a slushy, mushy love story! I couldn't let Ms. Frankton collect my paper. How could I explain to her that it wasn't really me who'd written about the love-crazy tadpoles? She'd never believe it was all the pen's fault. I hardly believed it myself. I had to dispose of the incriminating paper.

The bell rang. I leapt to my feet, scooped up my test paper, and scrambled for the door. I could pretend that in the rush to get outside I'd forgotten to hand it in. Ms. Frankton barked, "Brian-Hobble-sit-down-I-didn't-dismiss-you!"

"I have to go, ma'am."

"If you have to go, you have to go, Mr. Hobble, but if Nature has suddenly called you with an offer you can't refuse, kindly raise your hand and ask my permission before exiting this room with such unseemly haste."

I raised my hand. "Please can I be excused,

ma'am?" I called over my shoulder. I didn't wait for her answer. I just ran from the room. Outside, I crumpled my science test paper and tossed Giles and Miranda into the nearest garbage can. That was a mistake. You have to understand I was a little flustered. If I'd been thinking more clearly, I would have totally destroyed my incriminating story. I certainly would never have left it in a can so close to the classroom—where anybody could find it.

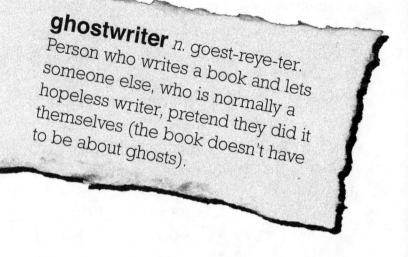

ghostwriter n. goest-reye-ter. Person who writes a book and lets someone else, who is normally a hopeless writer, pretend they did it themselves (the book doesn't have to be about ghosts).

"MAN, I was worried about you back there," said Vince Peretti at lunchtime. "I've never seen anyone go as white as you went. Not since I saw Jody Helmson looking at frog guts. What's going on?"

"I dunno," I said.

Vince scratched the back of his head through his thick curly hair. He avoided my eyes as he said, "By the way, Brian, don't get me wrong, but wearing that pen in your pocket makes you look like a nerd."

There was the Easyflow pen, back in the breast pocket of my shirt. I didn't remember putting it there, but somehow it managed to do things by itself. That pen was becoming a part of me now.

"Just thought, Brian, you know, your pen being

90

pink and all. You have to be careful around here, buddy. Kids might say you were . . . you know—not that there's anything wrong with that," he added quickly.

I pulled it out of my pocket. "It's not my pen, Vince," I said. "It belongs to Nathan Lumsdyke's mother."

"No kidding?" Vince was suddenly very interested. "Give me a look, Brian." I handed him the pen. Vince cradled it in his hands as if it were made of Zoggian cybernite (which, in case you didn't know, is the most valuable substance in the universe). "Awesome!" he breathed.

"It's only a pen, isn't it, Vince? I mean, is there something special about it?"

"If it belongs to Nathan's mother, it's real special."

"Why?"

"Brian, don't you know who Nathan Lumsdyke's mother is?"

"Mrs. Lumsdyke?" I said.

"She's Veronica Lovelace. She writes romantic novels."

"Really, Vince?"

"Have a look in the bookstore—there's a whole shelf of them: *Passionate Whispers*, *Love Among the Elms*, *My Pirate My Darling*, *Kisses at*

Midnight . . . We've got the full set at our house. My mom buys them all the time."

"Does she?"

"I flip through them too sometimes." Vince smiled shyly and did that head-scratching thing again. "Man, those love scenes are hot."

This was getting really spooky. "She must be a real quick writer," said Vince. "A new Veronica Lovelace book comes out every month."

I thought of the way the purple ink slid out of that Easyflow pen, filling up page after page without the slightest effort.

"Mom thinks she uses a ghostwriter," said Vince.

I had to take a deep breath before stuttering out, "G-Ghostwriter?"

"Probably lots of people use ghostwriters," continued Vince, "like Herbie Galanos did."

"Who's Herbie Galanos?" I asked.

"Pacific Kickboxing champion," said Vince. "I read his life story, *Doing It Tough*. I don't think Herbie wrote the book himself, but—"

"How do you know?" I asked.

"Herbie says he only went to school for three weeks in his whole life. He got suspended for headbutting his kindergarten teacher when she wouldn't let him eat the Play-Doh. He never went back to school."

Dreams
(Jan 14)

I watch a
pen write
a story
on its
own
...?!

"So no way could he write a whole book by him-self?" I said.

"'Course not," said Vince. "Especially after he broke all his fingers in his fight with Chutik Srinipat in Bangkok. And at the start of the book Herbie says, 'Thanks to Algernon Butterbottom for his help with this book.' If you ask me, this Algernon's the real writer. Herbie paid him a few grand, told him his story, and got old Algy to put it in a book. Mom says that's what you call a ghostwriter."

"But if Veronica Lovelace can really write, she wouldn't need a ghostwriter," I said.

"She would if she's real busy," said Vince. "Mom thinks she might just make up the basic stories and send them out to ghostwriters to write down. As long as they write the way she does, no one will know, except Veronica."

And the ghostwriters, I thought.

I wondered how Veronica Lovelace would find her ghostwriters. I mean, she'd call them up or send them an e-mail or something, wouldn't she? Or would she get her son, Nathan Lumsdyke, to lend them an Easyflow pen in class? "Speedy Peretti! Ice Man!" Mr. Quale was calling us from the gym. "Over here, pronto—you guys are later than the all-night bus."

"Post-Game Analysis," I said.

"Nearly forgot it," said Vince.

Mr. Quale had called a special meeting of the soccer team in his office. We were going to have a tactics talk to discuss what we needed to improve from the last game and to plan the strategy for the next one.

It was a bit of a squeeze in Mr. Quale's office. All the sports gear was stored there, on shelves around Mr. Quale's desk. What little wall space was left had sheets of butcher's paper with diagrams of soccer tactics and a poster of the Brazilian team, who Mr. Quale believed would beat the U.S. team in the next World Cup.

Most of the team were already inside, jostling among the basketballs and volleyball nets to find a comfortable spot to sit. As I walked in the door I found my hand clipping the pink Easyflow pen into the breast pocket of my shirt. When I saw Kelvin Moray look up, I unhooked it and pushed it deep down. I could get rid of that pen whenever I wanted. I'd do it some time soon. Not right now.

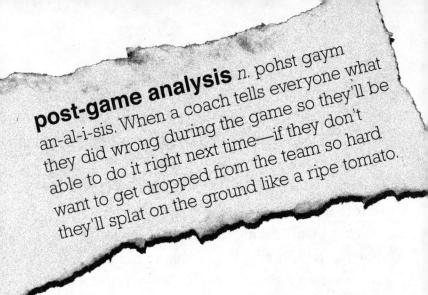

post-game analysis n. pohst gaym an-al-i-sis. When a coach tells everyone what they did wrong during the game so they'll be able to do it right next time—if they don't want to get dropped from the team so hard they'll splat on the ground like a ripe tomato.

IT was hard to say why the fight started. Usually teams are in a great mood after a win like we'd had on Friday. Kids who are deadly enemies put their arms around each other and tell each other how great they are, and how lucky they feel to have each other as friends and teammates. Locker-room fights normally break out only when you've lost. So it was strange that this team meeting turned so nasty.

It started in a normal enough way, with Mr. Quale giving his Post-Game Analysis. "Five things won that game for us on Friday, boys. Guts, guts, guts, guts, and finally, more guts!"

Mr. Quale's speeches before, during, and after our games were famous throughout the school for their colorful language. He wasn't bad on the tricky details of soccer tactics, but Mr. Quale was a total genius when it came to talking like a real coach.

"We've never been the most talented team in the division, but a champion team will beat a team of champions. In those last few minutes when everyone was tired, we were . . . " (here he referred to his notebook) " . . . we were tougher than crocodile-skin underpants."

Mr. Quale could think up the best expressions, which he scribbled in his notebook to read to us later. He had invented special names for everybody on the team. I'd been Mr. Invisible up until now, 'cause nobody noticed me on the field. Now I was the Ice Man, and I liked that better. Vince was Speedy because he was small but quick. Mario "Superglue" Fenton was great at sticking to opposition strikers. Then there were Sandbag, Rocco, Knobbly Knees, and Tangles. Mr. Quale called big Arthur Neerlander the Incredible Bulk. Kelvin Moray was always showing off on the soccer field, so he called him Show Pony.

First in Post-Game Analysis came praise for the things we'd done right. "Great effort at the back by Rocco and Bulk to hold off their attack all game. Sure we had some luck, but we earned it. And Brian Hobble was the Ice Man slotting home

BRIAN HOBBLE'S SOCCER tip
Nº 4
(How to defend penalties)

① Steal ball

② Hide it

③ Replace ball with heavy Rock

④ Watch the face of the other player ...!#

the penalty." Mr. Quale checked the notebook again. "This kid is cooler than a nudist at the North Pole!" He ruffled my hair.

There was applause from the team, but I noticed that Kelvin Moray didn't clap and dug his elbow into Rocco Ferris's ribs to stop him clapping, too.

"Brian Hobble was just lucky," said Kelvin.

"What's that supposed to mean, Kelvin?" asked Mr. Quale.

"Well, sir, it was a real useless penalty kick he did, sir. Their goalie should've stopped it easy, sir."

"Brian sucked him in," said Vince Peretti.

"Brian couldn't suck in a strawberry milkshake," said Kelvin. "He's the worst player on this team."

"At least he's not a big mouth like you," snapped Vince.

Mr. Quale stepped in to stop the argument from getting any more heated. "That'll do, Speedy Peretti! Boys, we don't need to fight about this. It was my call to let Brian take the penalty, and he didn't let us down. Any kick that scores a goal is good enough in my book, and Brian's kick won us the game. That's not to say there aren't areas of our play we need to improve on."

Mr. Quale opened the notebook again and announced in a deep, doom-laden voice, "The Soccer Hall of Shame!"

This was the bit I really looked forward to. In the Soccer Hall of Shame, Mr. Quale told us things we did wrong in a game. The Hall of Shame consisted mainly of abuse. Vicious, verbal, humiliating, personal insults handed out to each and every kid on the team for mistakes he'd made during the game. We loved it. Of course, Mr.

Quale was careful not to insult us within hearing of any parents, or Mrs. Davenport either, when she was acting as linesman. But behind the closed doors of his office, he really went to town: "Tangles, I've seen a three-legged tortoise dragging a ball and chain run faster than you!" (laughter). Tangles blushed deep crimson, then he laughed, too.

"Defense, Rocco, and Knobbly Knees, you let their forward slip between you like a greased worm on roller blades. I've seen bags of cement tackle with more commitment than you guys. As a matter of fact, I've got two bags of cement coming to training tomorrow to try out for your spots on the team!" Kelvin giggled and dug Rocco in the ribs. Rocco grinned.

"Kelvin Moray, our resident Show Pony," Mr. Quale went on, "if your brains were made of dynamite, they wouldn't blow your hat off!" Now Rocco dug Kelvin in the ribs. Kelvin scowled.

"There was a forward called Fernando Nunez who played for Brazil in the eighties," said Mr. Quale. (He knew heaps about old Brazilian soccer stars.) "Nunez had the skill of the great Pelé, but he refused to pass the ball. Eventually manager Roberto Santos lost patience and dropped him."

Kelvin looked puzzled. He didn't know where

Mr. Quale's history lesson was heading.

"Soccer is a team game, Kelvin. If you hog the ball like it's the last cupcake at a kindergarten birthday party, defenders can pick you off like a petunia in a flower pot."

"Petunia!" snickered Arthur Neerlander. He dug Kelvin in the ribs from the other side. Kelvin Moray was looking pretty uncomfortable now.

"Kelvin, you didn't pass to Brian Hobble once all day. When the ball did come to him, Brian gave us a great run down the wing and set up a goal. For heaven's sake, son, spread the ball wide and use Brian Hobble!"

"Brian's pathetic," muttered Kelvin. "And you should let me take the penalties next time, sir. The coach oughta go to his best player."

Mr. Quale stared at him. Coaches don't like being challenged by kids on their team. "Brian Hobble was my best player," said Mr. Quale quietly. "His good play earned the opportunity, and it was his cool head that converted it. Now shut up about that blasted penalty."

It was stuffy in the little office. The atmosphere was as tense as Captain Loopy's spaceship when the crew found they'd be out of oxygen in sixteen seconds. I tried to take off a bit of pressure. "Maybe I was a bit lucky, sir," I said. "Someone

else can take the penalty if we get one in the final."

"See?" said Kelvin. "The little weed is scared stiff he'll miss next time."

Mr. Quale fixed Kelvin with a gaze that would have withered the toughest Zoggian Death Fighter. His voice dripped liquid polynitrate (the coldest substance in the universe, according to Captain Loopy). He said, "Kelvin, forget last week's penalty. Start concentrating on how you're going to play the final. Don't be such a sniveling smear of snail snot."

Everyone roared with laughter and even Rocco Ferris couldn't help giggling. Arthur Neerlander howled, "Snail snot! Snail snot!" Until a gob of something like snail snot shot out of his own nose onto Kelvin Moray's knee. Kelvin really lost it then. He jumped to his feet, upsetting a box of basketballs and sending them tumbling around the office. He yelled at Mr. Quale, "You shouldn't have said that! You're not allowed to call me that!"

"Now, calm down, Kelvin," said Mr. Quale. "Drop it there, son."

"You think just 'cause you're a teacher you can say anything you like. Well, I don't have to take that from anyone. I can report you to Mrs.

Davenport. When she hears what you called me, you won't be coaching soccer at this school ever again!" With that, he ran out of the office.

There was a stunned silence, like in *Escape from Planet Zog* when Captain Loopy tells the crew he's resigning and leaving his potted plant Leafy in command of the ship.

Then Mr. Quale said, "That'll do, boys. Post-Game Analysis over. He'll be all right when he's cooled off a bit. We've got more important things to worry about than Kelvin Moray's little tantrums."

He was right, as it turned out. I was soon going to have something else to worry about myself.

dumbfound *v.t.* dum-found.
Make a stupid person very
surprised.

"CONGRATULATIONS are in order," said Mr.
Mackington at the start of our English class the
next morning. "Lancelot Cummins has chosen a
few students from all levels in the school to form a
Special Interest Writing Group. The Special
Interest Writers will be working with Mr.
Cummins over the next couple of days, developing
their writing. I'm pleased to announce that this
class will be represented by Nathan Lumsdyke . . ."

"Yes!" said Nathan, punching the air, and turning around as if to say to everyone, "I told you so
—actually."

Mr. Mackington led a brief round of applause,
but then went on, " . . . and Cassandra Wyman."
There was more polite clapping; Cassandra smiled
modestly. Nathan went over to her and shook her
hand in both of his. I thought he held it a
bit too long. Cassandra didn't seem to mind.

Mr. Mackington wasn't finished yet. "And also selected to join the Special Interest Writing Group is . . . Brian Hobble." For a moment the classroom was silent. Everybody was in shock. I was in shock. Lancelot Cummins had selected *me* as a Special Interest Writer!

All eyes turned to look at me. The silence was broken by a slow handclap . . . then another, and another. One by one, the class joined in as the clapping grew to a deafening roar. Mr. Mackington beamed as he marched down the aisle to my desk and shook me warmly by the hand. "Fantastic work, Brian. Selected for Special Interest Writing Group! I always knew you had the talent." Even Kelvin Moray and his friends were caught up in the general excitement. The girls were screaming out a chant, "Bri-an Hob-ble! Spe-cial Inter-est Wri-ter!"

All the kids were on their feet, yelling and slapping my back and cheering me on. Music from the Garunga District School Orchestra swelled, filling the room. Hands lifted me high and in a moment I was standing on my desk, looking down on the adoring faces of my classmates. I allowed myself to take an elegant bow.

Cassandra Wyman, eyes shining, could contain herself no longer. She threw her arms around my neck and planted a huge kiss on my cheek, sighing breathlessly into my ear, "Oh, Brian! Oh, Brian, you're a Special Interest Writer!"

As if! Did you really believe that would happen? Did I suck you in? Did you really think kids in our class would be impressed with me getting selected for Special Interest Writing Group? Instead, Mr. Mackington's stunning news was greeted by a couple of unenthusiastic claps, followed by the usual "Derrrr!" from the Kelvin Moray gang.

"Brian Hobble," said Mr. Mackington, "you may be surprised to be chosen for Mr. Cummins's writing group—you've been hiding your writing talent from us. But you're lucky that one of your fellow students rescued this from the garbage."

To my horror, Mr. Mackington pulled from his briefcase six sheets of crumpled paper. The flowery purple writing that covered them was too horribly familiar. Mr. Mackington smoothed out the sheets on the desk and cleared his throat.

In *My Mom's a Zombie Killer*, there's a real scary moment when the hero, Jake, discovers his English teacher is a flesh-eating zombie who wants to suck out his brains. I felt like that now. Mr. Mackington was going to read my tadpole story out loud! I wasn't as lucky as Jake. There was no chance of my mom swinging in —

through the classroom window on a rope the way Jake's mom had done, and driving a sharpened whiteboard marker through my teacher's heart.

"This is an unusual piece of work, Brian," said Mr. Mackington, "though I'm not sure that a science test was the right place to write it. You showed you know a lot about the life cycle of the frog. On the other hand, you only answered question one, so Ms. Frankton says she won't be able to pass you on the test.

"Nevertheless, we encourage creativity at this school and you've written something quite extraordinary. I'm delighted that Mr. Cummins's visit to our school has been such an inspiration. Quite frankly, I never knew you had it in you."

I didn't know I had it in me either. I didn't have it in me. I glanced down at the pink Easyflow pen peeping up at me from my shirt pocket.

Mr. Mackington waved my test paper in front of the class. "Brian was a bit embarrassed about this story, but I think you all ought to hear what he's written. It may inspire some of you to try harder with your writing."

This was worse than having a flesh-eating zombie suck out my brains. Mr. Mackington read the whole of my tadpole love story, in all its horrible mushy, slushy Veronica Lovelace-style detail. Six hideous pages of the romantic adventures of a tadpole called Miranda as she battles for survival in a Garunga District School science classroom. Madeline Chubb started crying almost as soon as it began, when Miranda became the first of the tadpoles to turn into a frog, left her childhood sweetheart, Giles, and crawled out of Ms. Frankton's fish tank.

"Poor Giles," thought Miranda, so handsome, so good-hearted, so loving, so legless . . .

Vince and Sean Peters hooted at the part in the story where, one by one, the other tadpoles turned into frogs and each tried to marry Miranda. All eyes in the room were glued to Mr. Mackington as he read the exciting part where Miranda tries to rescue Giles, who was finally frogified, but got stuck in a jar by Rocco Ferris.

... Miranda held her breath as she hopped bravely along the shelf and down onto the table. She could see Giles's handsome chest straining against the glass, his beautiful clear eyes rolling wide with fear. The hideous boy-giant, Rocco, had forgotten his captive for the moment. He was absorbed in his task of firing a rubber band from his ruler at an ugly giant (called Kelvin) across the classroom. Miranda clung to the jar and wrapped her delicate arms around its cool smoothness. She pushed it, toward the edge of the table, with all the strength of her being. She pushed with a desperate passion. She pushed with every fiber in her body. She pushed with love ...

This was so totally embarrassing! The first chance I got, I was giving that Easyflow pen back to Nathan Lumsdyke. I sneaked a look around the room. Who was the traitor classmate who had found my story in the trash and given it to Mr. Mackington? Vince? One of Kelvin Moray's gang? I couldn't see any clue in the faces around me. Nobody was giving anything away. Nobody was looking at me. They were all gripped by the spell of my story.

Then Mr. Mackington reached the tragic ending. It was amazing. It was gut wrenching. It was sadder than the moment on Planet Zog when Captain Loopy says good-bye to Andrew the Android, knowing they will never meet again.

At the end of my story, Miranda distracted Ms. Frankton by hopping into her lunchbox and croaking, while her lover, Giles, leapt to freedom from the science lab window. Miranda was caught by Ms. Frankton and carried off to the certain death of the dissecting room.

> . . . Her heart was full of joy. Giles was safe. His new life was just beginning, as surely as hers was ending.

Madeline Chubb was in tears again, and this time Abby and Sarah and Sofie joined in. My story ended:

> *A little egg, abandoned by its mother, never knowing its father. A legless, wriggling tadpole, one among ten thousand. A frightened frog, hunted by all, and a gory end on a schoolkid's chopping board. The life cycle of the frog —sad, short . . . and strangely beautiful.*

I kind of choked up myself. I had to put my hands up to my temples and pretend to be concentrating, so no one could see the tears in my eyes. But through the slits in my fingers, I could see other kids doing the same. *It was totally freaky!* Mr. Mackington finished reading and solemnly laid the crumpled science test on my desk. "Well done indeed, Brian." He parted his hands to lead a round of applause. But he never brought them together again. A moment later Miranda, Giles, and the Special Interest Writing Group were sucked out of my brain as if I'd been attacked by a flesh-eating zombie.

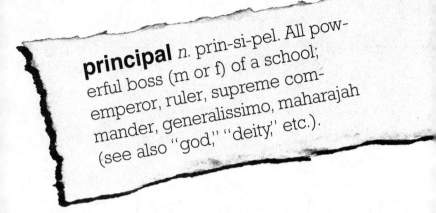

principal *n.* prin-si-pel. All powerful boss (m or f) of a school; emperor, ruler, supreme commander, generalissimo, maharajah (see also "god," "deity," etc.).

THE public-address speaker in the corner of the classroom crackled to life. The voice of our principal, Mrs. Davenport, rapped out sharply. "Listen please, students, and I'm sorry to interrupt your work, teachers . . . "

Mrs. Davenport's announcements were usually totally boring. "Interschool debaters, please wait for the bus at the Ogden Road gates at the end of lunchtime. The bike shed will remain off limits until the workmen finish removing the graffiti. The new Squeezee drinks will be available in the school cafeteria after Thursday . . . " Usually I paid no attention to the announcements. The next one sprang out of the speaker and grabbed me by the throat.

"Boys on Mr. Quale's soccer team are advised that Mr. Quale will not be at school today . . . "

Mr. Quale was not at school! Mrs. Davenport's voice went on. " . . . A parent has kindly offered to replace Mr. Quale at practice after school, so the team will meet on the playing field as planned."

I knew who was behind this, and he was a sniveling smear of snail snot.

Normally I was too intimidated by Kelvin Moray to face up to him. But now I was furious, and I had Vince with me for moral support. I pointed my finger at his chest.

"You reported Mr. Quale to Mrs. Davenport, didn't you?" I said.

Kelvin Moray didn't deny it. "Teachers are supposed to be responsible, Brian."

"Mr. Quale is a really responsible teacher," I said.

"Calling kids smears of snail snot isn't responsible. Teachers who call kids 'snail snot' deserve whatever's coming to them," he replied primly.

SCIENCE Breakthroughs BY B. HOBBLE

Flashlight

Gentle music

Trying to get a snail to slide backward along its trail . . .

. . . cutlery fence

7:25 pm
Tues.

"An insult like that could do permanent damage to my self-esteem."

"Your self-esteem needs as much damage as people can possibly do to it." It felt good to be talking back to Kelvin Moray, especially with Vince there to see me do it.

"You're not supposed to take things like that personally, Kelvin," said Vince. "You've heard Mr. Quale call us worse things than that after every game. He's only joking."

"Kelvin, give us a break," I said. "Mr. Quale is the best coach we've ever had. If Mrs. Davenport fires him, who's going to coach us for the final?"

Kelvin Moray smirked. (Thank you again, thesaurus. "Smirked" is a word that means he smiled in a superior way, like he had really high self-esteem, which in no way could even be scratched by being called "snail snot.")

"We'll get a new coach," said Kelvin, "Someone who really knows something about soccer."

"Who?"

"Someone with soccer brains. You can bet that the new coach won't let Brian Hobble take a penalty ever again."

"Who is it?"

"Someone who played in the pros for fifteen

years. Someone who won three championships and was runner-up twice."

"Who?" I'd guessed it already. Kelvin was always boasting about him.

"My dad," he said, and swaggered off with another smirk.

"Someone has to talk to Mrs. Davenport, Vince," I said.

"Not me, no way!" said Vince.

"You're the team captain."

"So?"

"Vince, the only way we'll get Mr. Quale back is if you talk to Mrs. Davenport and tell her the team believes in him and we need him for the final."

"Will you come with me, Brian?"

"Why?"

"You're better at talking."

"Are you scared of Mrs. Davenport, Vince?"

"Are you scared of her, Brian?"

"Yes," I said.

"Me, too," said Vince.

Even the teachers were scared of Mrs. Davenport. It was better to avoid attracting her attention. I'd only ever been sent to her office once. That was when I was caught climbing on the roof above the restrooms to get Sean Peters's model glider back. I knew it was off limits, but there wouldn't have been any problem if the stupid roof hadn't given way. It was just my bad luck to drop through into the girls' end. It was even worse luck to fall into a stall with Madeline Chubb in it. Mrs. Davenport hadn't been very understanding at the time.

I'd managed to stay out of her way since that unfortunate incident, but now Vince and I were in the lion's den, standing in front of her desk.

She wasn't a really large woman. But, even sitting down like she was now, she had a way of looking at you that made you feel smaller and her seem bigger. Right now I felt like Captain Loopy after the Zoggian Inquisitors force-fed him a tablet that shrank him to the size of a rabbit.

Mrs. Davenport's voice was as cold as steel monkey bars on a winter morning. "And just what gives you the impression that I've treated Mr. Quale unfairly, Brian Hobble?"

"Well, er . . . (cough) . . . um, he's nice, ma'am," I said.

"Real nice," added Vince.

"He's, um, a good soccer coach, too, ma'am," I said.

"Real good, ma'am," added Vince.

"And we're playing the district final on Friday," I said. "It's the first time Garunga Glory has ever made it, and we really need Mr.

Quale to give us a good pep talk at halftime. 'Cause if he doesn't, we'll lose for sure."

"For sure, ma'am," added Vince. Couldn't Vince think of anything more imaginative to say? I kicked his ankle. "Ow," added Vince.

"I see," said Mrs. Davenport. She rose majestically from behind her desk, like a Zoggian Starship pulling out of a space port. She towered over us. Now I felt like Captain Loopy after that second shrinking pill turned him into a slug. She said, "I'm pleased that you feel loyal enough to a member of our staff to deliver this glowing testimonial, boys. I take it other members of the team share your high opinion of Mr. Quale?"

"Only Kelvin Moray doesn't like him," I said.

Vince added, "And that's just 'cause they had a fight when Mr. Quale called Kelvin 'a sniveling smear of '—ow!" I kicked his ankle again. It would only make matters worse if Vince told Mrs. Davenport what Mr. Quale had called Kelvin.

Mrs. Davenport raised her eyebrows. She must have read Lancelot Cummins's books, too. If you painted her face green and shaved her head, she'd look exactly like a Zoggian Inquisitor. She had the expression perfect.

"So Mr. Quale referred to Kelvin Moray as a . . . um, in a derogatory manner?"

Suddenly Vince had plenty to say. "Kelvin was asking for it, ma'am," he said. "He thought he should have taken the penalty in the semi, even though Brian got it in anyway, so Kelvin really was being a sniveling smear of snail snot. Anyway, Mr. Quale always uses this real colorful language."

"Does he indeed?"

"We don't mind it, ma'am. He calls us stuff like that all the time."

"Such as?"

"Once when I missed a goal he called me a hopeless blob of jellyfish blubber."

"Did he now?" said Mrs. Davenport. A smile crawled out from the corner of her mouth like a Zoggian Cyberworm.

"And he said Mario Fenton was as useful as diarrhea at a scout camp," said Vince.

I wished Vince would shut up. He wasn't making things any better for Mr. Quale.

"And once Mr. Quale goes . . . "—here Vince launched into a very realistic impression of Mr. Quale's Post-Game Analysis—" 'Rocco, you've got the brains of a house brick,' and Rocco goes, 'That's not true, sir!' so Mr. Quale says, 'Sorry, Rocco, you're absolutely right. You haven't got the brains of a house brick!' "

Great Moments in Literature

© B. HOBBLE

*capsule not to scale

NormaLoopy

Loopy   RABBit   carroT

Vince thought this was all going down so well. He laughed loudly, and he didn't seem to notice that Mrs. Davenport wasn't laughing with him.

"Vincent, do you think this is how soccer coaches ought to be speaking to their players?"

"Oh, for sure, ma'am. For sure! On *The Big Game* on TV they take the cameras into the locker rooms at halftime. The language those coaches use is amazing."

Then Mrs. Davenport did something surprising. From the top drawer of her desk, she took two pens and two sheets of paper and handed them to us.

"I wonder if you boys would do something for me. Make a list of some of the colorful expressions you've heard from Mr. Quale."

"Now?"

"Yes, thank you, Vince."

"What if we can't think of any?" I asked.

"Vince just said he insults players all the time. There must be plenty of them you remember."

This was sounding really bad. I didn't want to get Mr. Quale into any more trouble. Vince was writing away, so I thought I'd better put some things down. But what? I wasn't going to say he told Rocco he was weaker than a limp noodle. Or that he once said, "Bulk Neerlander, if your brains were ink, there wouldn't be enough for a decent-sized period." Mrs. Davenport might think insults like that would damage Arthur Neerlander's self-esteem.

I tried to remember the good, encouraging things Mr. Quale told us. "Great goalkeeping, Sean

Peters. You stopped more shots than a duck in a shooting gallery." "Vince Peretti, you're a better dribbler than a baby with a melting ice cream."

I sneaked a look at Vince's paper. The idiot! Vince was filling his paper with insults from the Soccer Hall of Shame. He thought they were funny, but what would Mrs. Davenport think when she read that Mr. Quale had said things like, "Tangles, I walk through my garden on a rainy Sunday treading on things cleverer than you!" Or, "I've seen better legs than yours on my kitchen table." And worst of all, "Son, you couldn't kick a goal if it knelt down in front of you with its butt in the air."

After a few minutes, Mrs. Davenport said, "That's enough boys," and picked up our papers. Her face was as expressionless as a flesh-eating zombie as she read Vince's list of insults about beetle brains and vats of vampire vomit and butts in the air.

"Thank you for coming to see me, boys. You've been very helpful. You may go."

Vince still didn't get it. "So can Mr. Quale coach us this afternoon, ma'am?"

"I believe Mr. Quale is otherwise engaged this afternoon, Vince. But I understand Kelvin Moray's father has kindly volunteered to take over."

"But we don't know him, ma'am," I said.

"So?"

"Mr. Moray might be no good at coaching kids, ma'am. If he's not good at keeping control of the team, kids might sort of . . . well, mess it up for him."

Mrs. Davenport seemed to swell to the size of a Zoggian Superblimp. "Brian Hobble, nobody will

Interesting things at school
(by B. HoBBLE)

MRS. D.

I'm full of hot air today, boys...

mess up for Mr. Moray!" she boomed. "I shall personally observe this afternoon's practice. If I am not entirely satisfied with any boy's behavior, that boy will look like"—here she glanced at the insults Vince had written on his paper—"a small smidgen of pescorated pigeon poop when I've finished with him. Do I make myself clear, you"—another glance down—"woeful wriggling worms?"

She certainly did.

Outside her office I said, "You're an idiot, Vince; you know that?"

"What did I say?"

"Telling her all those things Mr. Quale says."

"Brian, you said we just had to tell her the truth."

"Everyone knows Mr. Quale isn't supposed to talk to kids like that, Vince. It doesn't matter whether we enjoy his insults or not. He was in enough trouble before. Now he'll be lucky if he keeps his job at the school."

Vince nodded gloomily. "Maybe Kelvin's dad will be a good coach. He must know something about soccer. Maybe he won't be at all like Kelvin. Maybe we'll really like him."

Yeah, dream on, Vince. It was time for another puff of the asthma spray.

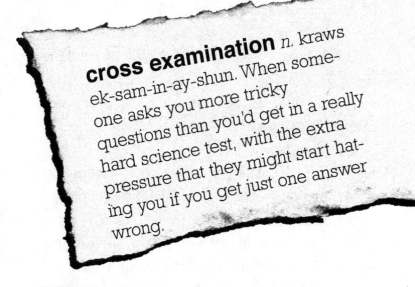

cross examination *n.* kraws ek-sam-in-ay-shun. When someone asks you more tricky questions than you'd get in a really hard science test, with the extra pressure that they might start hating you if you get just one answer wrong.

THEN I stuffed the spray quickly back into my pocket, because Cassandra Wyman was coming over to talk to me. This was something new.

"Brian, can I say something to you?"

"Er, sure, Cassandra."

Vince was watching, fascinated by this new phenomenon. His best friend, Brian Hobble, was talking to a girl!

"It's sort of private," said Cassandra.

"Oh, I get it," said Vince meaningfully. He sidled off slowly, looking back at me curiously. What could Cassandra Wyman possibly have to say to me that was private?

"I want to apologize to you, Brian."

"Oh, sure, no harm done, Cassandra," I said. (Apologize for what? I thought.)

"I didn't think . . ."

"It's all right, Cassandra." (What was she talking about?)

"I just really wanted you to get into Special Interest Writing Group."

"Oh, that," I said.

"But I swear, I had no idea Mr. Mackington would read your tadpole story aloud to the class. I hope you didn't mind."

"It was *you* who gave Mr. Mackington my story!" There was one mystery solved.

"I shouldn't have done it. But when I saw you throw your science test into the trash I wondered why. After I'd read a few lines, I couldn't stop. Brian, it was so fantastic! If you can really write like that, you have to be in Special Interest Writing Group. You'll be the best, I know."

She was smiling that smile again.

The Bone Suckers started turning my legs into jelly as I stammered out, "Yeah, it should be pretty good, working with Lancelot Cummins and all that. I'm looking forward to it."

There was an awkward pause, as if Cassandra was only now getting to the private bit of the conversation. She said, "Um . . . I don't know you all that well, Brian . . . "

I said, "Er, maybe not."

"And I was wondering . . . "

"Er . . . yeah?" This wasn't getting us very far.

Cassandra Wyman took a big breath in. Then she asked the crunch question. "Did you really write that tadpole story yourself, Brian?"

In *The Flushing*, the psychiatrist trying to find the cause of Zeke's toiletophobia straps him to a lie detector, which bleeps when Zeke's pulse rate goes up. The psychiatrist grills Zeke with embarrassing questions about his potty training and bed-wetting. It felt as if Cassandra Wyman had me strapped to a lie detector now.

Did I really write the tadpole story myself?

"Sort of," I said. (Half true. I had held the Easyflow pen and moved it around the paper— that was writing, wasn't it? Lie detector gives a little bleep, then settles down to a flat line.)

"You didn't, you know, copy it from a book or something?" she asked.

"No." (True. Lie detector flat again. Of course I hadn't copied it from a book! Where would I find a book about tadpoles in Ms. Frankton's science lab? Even Veronica Lovelace wouldn't write about that. So maybe that part of the story did come from me . . .)

"I never knew you were a talented writer."

"Neither did I." (True. Lie detector flat as the Nullarbor Plain.)

"Why didn't you ever write stories like that before?"

"I dunno." (False. Lie detector bleeps. I knew very well why I'd never written like that. Because I'd never had the Easyflow pen before.)

"Was it because you were scared?"

"Scared?" (Lie detector not sure whether to bleep or not.)

"You know, Brian, when you write something down, it tells everyone about the sort of person you are. Some people find that a bit scary."

"Really?" (Lie detector starts a series of short bleeps, wondering where this is leading.)

Cassandra laid a light hand on my bare elbow. The warmth of it was burning my skin. So that's what girl germs felt like—quite nice, really. I wouldn't be washing them off any time soon.

"I'm glad you're brave enough to show your feelings in your writing, Brian," she said. "Most boys think that's not cool. Like, boys aren't supposed to feel sorry for frogs, are they?"

"Er, no." (Absolutely true. Lie detector stops bleeping.)

"But you will write more stories, won't you,

B. HOBBLE'S
Heroic Moments
from the future

Excalibur
Sword

Rock

Cassandra
needs a
knife to
cut her
sandwich

Brian? 'Cause I'd really like to read them. You will write something really good in Special Interest Writing?"

As long as I used the Easyflow pen, that should be possible. If I dared to use it again, that is. Although it would be sort of like cheating on a test. But, if I didn't use it, I'd go straight back to my old hopeless-at-writing self—and look like a complete idiot in front of all the kids, Lancelot Cummins, *and* Cassandra. Without the Easyflow pen, Special Interest Writing Group would be a total disaster.

"Promise me you'll keep writing great stories, Brian," said Cassandra.

"I'm sure I will, Cassandra," I said. "I'm sure." (Lie detector bleeps loudly.)

I watched her move off toward the library.

"You're in love, aren't you, Brian?" said a quiet voice at my elbow. A cloud of Nutter Butter fumes drifted across my nostrils. Madeline Chubb. I always thought she was stupid. How could she possibly know something like that?

"You're in love with Cassandra Wyman," Madeline repeated.

"Am not," my mouth blurted out. (Lie detector goes psycho, screams at a million decibels, then explodes.)

physical training *n.* fi-sik-al tray-ning. Form of severe, agonizing, painful torture devised by people who never had to do it themselves when they were kids, or, if they did, they don't ever want to do it again.

AFTER school, I jogged out to the oval for our first soccer practice with Mr. Moray. I found it hard to jog in a straight line. Sean Peters was running beside me, leaning in on me, his motor-mouth working nonstop.

"Brian, you know who we're playing against in the district final? Eastburn Eagles. They beat Pettering Pelicans four–two in their semi, so they must have a pretty good attack. And Brian, don't you think we should play an extra defender to neutralize their forward strength? 'Cause Eastburn let in two goals, so that means they must have a weakness in defense, don't you think, Brian? So you and Speedy Peretti should play way up the ground, Brian, to pounce on the loose ball, don't you think, Brian?"

Mr. Quale used to call Sean Peters Seven Eleven because he was like an all-night store and never shut up. This afternoon, of course, there would be no Mr. Quale. Mr. Moray would be arriving soon to coach us instead.

To kill time, Sean and Vince and I practiced taking penalties. I took three firm steps up to the penalty spot and slammed a vicious laser-rocket kick into the bottom corner of the net.

Sean dived full length across the goal line. "Saved it!" he gasped.

"No, you didn't," I said.

"I did too save it, Brian," said Sean. "I just reached it with the fingertips of my left hand and deflected it past the post."

"Shut up, Seven Eleven. It was a goal!"

"Was not!"

"Was too."

"Was not, Brian!"

"Was too, Sean!"

That was the trouble playing soccer with an imaginary ball. There were too many arguments.

The real balls were still in the office by the locker rooms. We weren't allowed to get them. Supercoach Mr. Moray was getting changed in there. Mr. Quale used to get changed in the office, too, but first he always kicked a few balls on to the field for us to warm up with. Mr. Moray apparently didn't think of doing this. So we had to wait for him.

There was only one ball on the field. Kelvin Moray had brought his ball from home and was down in the far goal, practicing penalties with Rocco Ferris. They wouldn't let anyone else play with them. It was boring. Arthur Neerlander and Mario Fenton stood on the sideline and started a spitting competition to see who could spit the farthest.

Finally Mr. Moray came out of the office, carrying a fat, bulging bag of soccer balls. Mr. Moray was fat and bulging, too. If he'd really been a champion player, it must have been many years ago. Judging from the size of his stomach, he'd spent a lot of the time since then eating Macho Burgers with double fries and chocolate milkshakes. That red sweatsuit he was wearing didn't help. It made his face look even redder and the waistband was threatening to bust.

If the body-invading aliens from *Brown Gunk from Mars* ever moved into his beer gut, they'd be able to build a mansion with six bedrooms and five bathrooms. And a swimming pool.

Mr. Moray blew a whistle. "In here, boys." We jogged dutifully across to him.

Training with Mr. Quale was fun. He cracked jokes, abused us when we did something wrong, ran drills and exercises that gave everybody equal time with the ball, abused us again. He organized knockout competitions, three a side, for dribbling and shooting and tackling. He was very fair and always encouraged us, especially kids who weren't so good. He made a game out of fitness training, so we hardly realized how tired we were until it was over. Even if he thought a kid was being slack, he'd punish him by making him do some funny

WHAT coaches are like when they're at home... (Eg. ③ MR. MCKAY)

I should have bought the super-strength version!!

exercise like pushing the ball across the field with his nose.

Training under Mr. Moray was different. There was no fun.

"Warm up," he growled. "Six laps around the field. Go!" He blew a whistle. While we set off to puff around the ground, he scribbled notes in a notebook.

I have to admit, as a team we weren't really fit. Vince Peretti was the only one of us able to run the whole way. By the time we'd run twice around the ground, he'd done it three times and was starting to lap people. Arthur Neerlander and Sean Peters stopped running after half a lap and started walking.

I managed four laps without stopping, then got a stitch in my side. For a while I made sure I did my walking when I was on the far end of the field and broke into a trot when I got close to Mr. Moray. He didn't seem to be paying any attention to us anyway. He was just scratching away at his paper.

When we staggered back, and one by one collapsed on the ground beside him, he read out what he'd written. "Soccer is a game of strategy. Our best player is Kelvin, so our strategy will be to kick the ball to Kelvin. Kelvin's strategy will be, score the goals."

Vince and I looked at each other. We thought a new coach might have had something more sophisticated to say.

"Practice drill," said Mr. Moray. "Backs against forwards. Forwards, pass when I blow the whistle. Backs, tackle when I blow the whistle twice. I blow the whistle three times, everybody stops and listens."

Vince and I were the wing forwards. We had to take the ball down the sidelines, then pass it in to Kelvin at the top of the penalty area. Kelvin had to get it past the fullbacks and kick a goal. Mr. Moray made us do the drill about three squillion times. Kelvin slotted in goal after goal. It wasn't hard. It was only Sean Peters in the net, and half the time Sean fell over and missed the ball, even if Kelvin's shot was a feeble dribbler.

Each time Kelvin scored, Mr. Moray would blow his whistle and say, "Good work, Kelvin. Rest of you, remember that." If one of the backs beat Kelvin in the tackle, Mr. Moray would blow his whistle three times to stop the game. Then he'd criticize me or Vince for a bad pass, or he'd call a foul tackle on the defender. Or both.

After half an hour and seventeen squillion

drills, even Kelvin was getting bored. "Can we practice some penalties now, Dad?" he asked.

Mr. Moray blew the whistle three times. "Good idea, Kelvin. Penalties. Goalie, into the net."

Sean Peters shuffled over to stand on the goal-line.

Mr. Moray lined up five balls beside the penalty spot. "All right, Kelvin. Five out of five."

Vince put up his hand. "Excuse me, Mr. Moray; usually Brian Hobble takes the penalties for Garunga."

Mr. Moray said, "Not any more, he doesn't."

Vince persisted, "Brian's got the coolest head on the whole team, sir. Mr. Quale calls him the Ice Man."

Mr. Moray said, "I'm coaching today, boy. Kelvin takes the penalties."

He turned back to the penalty spot. "Kelvin, five out of five. Rest of you, fitness drill. Ten jumping jacks, ten push-ups, ten squats, then repeat. Go."

Kelvin began to boot penalty shots at Sean. Sean was making a big effort to make Kelvin look bad, and he saved the first two before Kelvin finally hit one past him. The rest of the team half-heartedly dragged themselves to their feet and started lazy jumping jacks. I took a puff on my asthma inhaler.

Mr. Moray was writing in his notebook again—or trying to. He seemed to be having trouble with his pen. He tapped it on the notebook, flicked it a few times, then noticed me puffing on my inhaler. He pointed a pudgy finger at me. "You, boy."

I pointed a skinny finger at me. "Me, sir?"

"Yes, you, boy."

"I, me, sir." (I was getting the hang of talking to Mr. Moray.)

"You doing what, boy?"

I patted my chest. "Asthma, sir. Exercise. Can't breathe."

He pointed in the direction of the locker rooms. "Spare pen. My bag. Office."

I pointed to the office.

"Bag, sir?"

"Bring here, boy."

"Bag, sir?"

"Pen, boy. In bag."

"Pen, sir."

I jogged over toward the office. Mr. Moray turned his attention to the team and was coaching Rocco Ferris through his push-ups. "Chest to ground! One-and-two-and-three-and . . ." He wasn't watching me.

Then I had a brilliant idea. At least, it seemed like a brilliant idea at the time . . .

When I got back to Mr. Moray, he was congratulating Kelvin on his penalties. "Three from five. Can do better."

"Yes, Dad," said Kelvin.

"Five more," said Mr. Moray.

He noticed me standing beside him.

"Yes, boy?"

"Pen, sir."

He took it without thanking me. Or looking at me. Or looking at the pen I brought him.

The rest of the team had finished their exercises and were milling around, red-faced and panting. They hoped the next part of practice would at least be more fun. But Mr. Moray clearly didn't believe in fun.

"Cross-country run," he snapped. "Everybody. Down to river, Hordern Street bridge, follow bike track, around the Ern Smith Reserve, back here. Timing you. Go!" He checked his watch and blew his whistle. As we trotted away, I saw him start writing in his notebook.

I hate cross-country runs. Give me a choice between doing a cross-country run and being tortured by Zoggian Inquisitors and I'd take the Zoggian dungeon every time.

The track leading out of the school and through

the Urban Forest was slippery with mud and over-grown with wet grass. By the time I got to the river, my legs were soaked and freezing water was running down my calves into my socks. Next came the Hordern Street bridge. Vince Peretti was already across it and heading down the bike track when I got to the bottom of the steps. Other kids were strung out behind him. Most were well in front of me. They'd all done the hard bridge-climbing bit. I still had to climb the eighty-nine quintillion steps going up and another eighty-nine quintillion coming down to the bike track on the other side of the river. My legs seemed to be made of watery porridge.

Only Sean Peters was lagging behind the field. I caught up with him as he stopped to pull up his socks. Even he was having trouble talking. "I thought (puff) Mr. Moray (puff) would've been a (puff) better coach than that (puff), don't you think (puff), Brian? He sort of (puff) favors Kelvin a bit (puff), don't you (puff) think?"

Sean and I walked across the bridge and down onto the bike track along the river. It wasn't really a bike track anymore. It hadn't had anything with wheels travel along it for about a hundred years. Tree roots had buckled the blacktop into a treach-erous obstacle course of cracks and bulges that

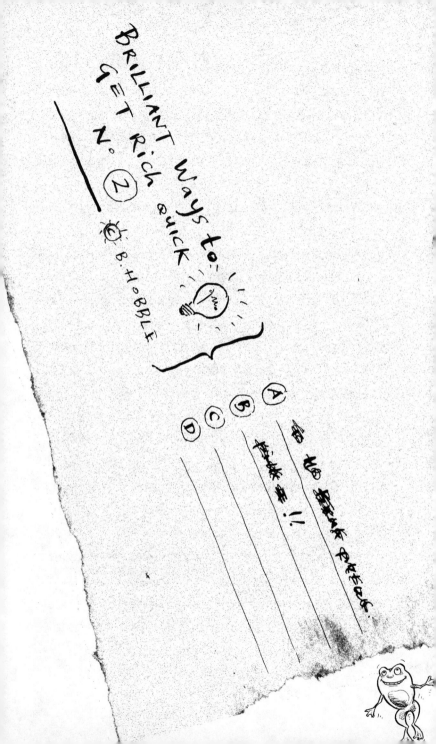

tried their best to trip you up. If you fell on that deadly track, you'd be ripped open by crack edges as sharp as the fangs of a Zoggian Guard Dragon. At the end of the bike track the route turned right and led to Ern Smith Reserve. It was all uphill.

My lungs were bursting. I was ready to stop. I was ready to die. But I ran on. I had to live. I had to keep running. I had to get back to practice. I was determined to be there for Mr. Moray's strategy talk. I took a quick puff on my asthma inhaler and, performance enhanced, I staggered on.

When we got back from the run, Mr. Moray was no longer alone. Mrs. Davenport had joined him.

"Team talk," called Mr. Moray. "All in here. Principal wants to address you."

Mrs. Davenport said, "On behalf of Garunga Glory, I just want to thank Mr. Moray for giving up his time to take on this job. We're always very grateful to parents who help around the school, and we all appreciate it very much." She led us in a round of applause.

"Now Mr. Moray has a few thoughts for us about the final on Friday, and I'm sure we'll all be very interested in what he has to tell us."

"Er, right," said Mr. Moray. He opened his notebook and started to read:

Soccer is a game of strategy . . .

"just like love," sighed Crystal Claire,
brushing a lock of auburn hair from her
perfect heart-shaped face . . .

We all stared at Mr. Moray. Mrs. Davenport stared at Mr. Moray. Mr. Moray stared at his notebook. He couldn't take his eyes off it. And he couldn't stop himself from reading out loud.

. . . Aurelio Gucci appeared at the locker
room door. His chest was heaving. Steam
rose from his broad shoulders. Nuzzling
her pretty nose into the emblem on his
soccer shirt, Crystal tilted her face to gaze
up into his. "My darling, Aurelio!"
whispered Crystal, "My own sweet left
midfielder!" Their lips met in the gentlest
of kisses . . .

In Lancelot Cummins's book *A T-Rex Ate My Homework*, Miss Weevil opens her teacher's desk and finds it crawling with baby stegosaurs. Her lips quiver feverishly and the color drains from her face, leaving a deathly pallor. When I first read that sentence I hadn't been sure what a "deathly pallor" was. Now I knew. There was a deathly pallor on Mr. Moray's face and his lips were quivering feverishly. He flipped over the page in the notebook. And another, and another . . . his voice sounded like Miss Weevil's did when a baby stegosaur leaps into her mouth and gets stuck in her throat.

"Errr . . . egglugg-eee . . . okkk!" he said.

Mrs. Davenport grabbed the notebook from him and flipped a page or two herself. It was apparently full of mushy stuff. Mrs. Davenport did her Zoggian swelling act. Before our eyes, Mr. Moray seemed to shrink before her withering gaze, like a slug under a bucketful of salt.

"What is the meaning of this?" she thundered.

The baby stegosaur was still stuck in Mr. Moray's throat. "Errr, gee-uggee . . . erkkk," he said.

Mr. Moray grabbed the notebook back from Mrs. Davenport and snapped it shut. His face lost its deathly pallor and began turning back to its usual red. "Urgent appointment," he muttered. Fat though he was, Mr. Moray almost ran to the office. The door slammed shut behind him.

The team shuffled nervously, looking to Mrs. Davenport to tell them what to do next. "I think

Close-up

practice is over for today, boys," said Mrs. Davenport. "I shall inform you tomorrow about the schedule for future practice sessions."

Kids sidled off toward the locker rooms. They couldn't believe what had just happened and nobody had the slightest idea what had caused it.

But I did. I recognized only too well the style of that flowery purple writing. I'd seen something peeping out of the trouser pocket of Mr. Moray's red sweatsuit. It was the pink end of the Easyflow pen.

We'd all showered and changed by the time Mr. Moray emerged from the office. He was wearing a suit now, but the collar was turned up and his tie was crooked. He still looked very shaken. He didn't say anything to any of us, and even to Kelvin he just said, "Home, Kelvin. Now." He hustled Kelvin out the school gates and into a smooth silver car. They drove away.

The office door was wide open. I ducked inside. I had to get that pen back. Having that Easyflow pen had turned out to be quite useful. (1) It had gotten Cassandra Wyman to talk to me and (2) it had gotten rid of the soccer coach from hell.

Now I needed it to do one more job for me—the most important so far. That Easyflow pen was going to write something impressive to get me through Special Interest Writing Group. The pen had got me into that mess, and I was counting on it to get me out of it, too. After that I'd give it back to Nathan Lumsdyke, and go back to being the old unimaginative Brian Hobble.

But first I had to find it. It wasn't on the desk, or in any of the drawers. Surely Mr. Moray wouldn't have taken it away with him. After what had just happened, he'd be wanting to get rid of it as soon as possible. The wastepaper basket by the desk was overflowing with pages ripped from a notebook. Crumpled-up pages covered with flowery purple writing. Pages and pages of tender embraces, strong hairy arms, and heaving bosoms. And kissing.

Under the crumpled balls of paper, at the bottom of the basket, I found the Easyflow pen. Someone had stomped on it with a large soccer cleat. It was smashed into a zillion pieces.

My chances of writing something to impress Cassandra and Lancelot Cummins were in a zillion pieces, too.

"Hey, it's the Ice Man!" I whipped around. Mr. Quale was back.

How to IMPRESS Girls
(by B. HoBBLE) ©!!

Step ① Borrow Poetry Books

Hamlet
WB Yeats Collected Works

Step ② When Cassandra walks past, pretend they fall out of your bag...

← quietly knee your bag...

PATH WALKING Cassandra's

Step ③ Act like you didn't see her...

(eg. whistling is good!)

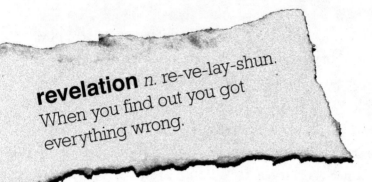

revelation n. re-ve-lay-shun.
When you find out you got
everything wrong.

"I'M glad I caught you, Ice Man," said Mr. Quale. "I wanted to have a word before practice tomorrow."

"You mean, you'll be at practice tomorrow, sir?"

"Of course I will be, Brian, and so will you if you want to keep your spot on the team."

"So you got your coaching job back, sir?"

Mr. Quale rubbed his chin. "Was I supposed to have lost it?"

I didn't know what to say to this. He must have noticed he'd been fired this morning. My mouth got ahead of my brain again and gushed, "I thought, that is, Vince and me thought . . . when you called Kelvin Moray 'snail snot,' and he lost it and reported you to Mrs. Davenport and then his dad took over, well, we thought when you missed practice . . . "

"You thought what, Brian?"

I knew I wasn't making much sense. "Vince Peretti and I went to see Mrs. Davenport," I said.

"Yes, she told me about your curious social visit. She said you had some nice things to say about me, too."

"We tried not to get you into trouble, sir. We know you're not supposed to call kids names, but we don't mind really. We like the things you call us. But she made us write down all the stuff you said."

"You wrote it down?"

"I just put down the good things you said, sir. But Vince put . . . well, she might somehow have found out some Hall of Shame insults, too. Mrs. Davenport's got this way of getting stuff out of you, even if you try not to tell her . . . "

Mr. Quale didn't seem at all concerned. Instead, he roared with laughter. "So the old buzzard got you to write down my most memorable quotes? Isn't she a sneaky slurp of slug slime!"

I was surprised to hear him calling a school principal a "slurp of slug slime."

"You mean, you won't get in trouble with Mrs. Davenport for calling us those things?"

Mr. Quale pulled his notebook from the drawer on his desk. "Brian, Mrs. Davenport can be scary when she wants to be. It's a useful talent for a school principal to have. But she enjoys a laugh, too. She's come up with some of my best expressions—look."

The notebook was divided into two columns marked Q and D.

"Mrs. Davenport and I have a sort of competition, to see who can think up the best insults. It's like a little game we play. She's always interested in knowing what I say behind the closed door in my Post-Game Analysis. She needs a few good insults to throw at us teachers in staff meetings. If she comes up with a good one, I note it down, under D for Davenport."

In the notebook's Q column were some of the expressions we'd heard from Mr. Quale, but I was surprised to see that under D were plenty that I recognized, too. Even "sniveling smear of snail snot" was under D.

"Did Mrs. Davenport think up that one?" I asked.

Mr. Quale smiled. " 'Sniveling smear of snail snot' was what she called Mr. Mackington when he complained about the cheap staff-room coffee. It seemed too good to waste, so I put it into my Hall of Shame book."

It was a new idea to me, that teachers went around insulting each other. But I was still curious about something else. "Then, if Mrs. Davenport didn't fire you from coaching us, why weren't you at practice today, sir?"

"Ah, that's exactly what I wanted to talk to you about, Brian." He unrolled a poster and stuck it on the wall. It showed a black soccer player with frizzy gray hair in a green and yellow sweatsuit. Underneath the picture it said:

COACHING THE COACHES—
clinics with Roberto Santos

"Roberto Santos is a legend in Brazil," said Mr. Quale. "One of the great coaches. He's in town for a few days, with a couple of his up-and-coming players. They're running clinics to give coaches like me a few pointers. I didn't think I'd get in, but, when they accepted me, I wasn't going to miss it, even in the week of the district final." So that was it. Mr. Quale hadn't been fired as coach at all. Vince and I had been through the agony of that horrible Mrs. Davenport interview for nothing.

"I learned a lot at the clinic today," said Mr. Quale. "Some technical tactics, but Santos had a lot to say about getting a team to work together. Garunga Glory has to work together if we're going to win that final. We can't have Kelvin Moray feeling that I haven't been fair to him."

"That wasn't your fault, sir."

"It doesn't matter whose fault it was. I need Kelvin to feel happy to be on the team. Tomorrow I want to settle this business of who's our best penalty-taker in a way that satisfies all parties."

"Kelvin can take them, sir," I said.

"I think you can beat him, Brian. If you're the better penalty-taker, that's what the team needs. So I'm proposing a shoot-out at practice. Ten penalties each, and the winner becomes our penalty-kicker for the final. That sound fair?"

BRIAN HOBBLE'S SOCCER TIPS
No. 5
How to take penalties...

(A) Imagine you're a Giant
(B) Imagine the goalie is a rabbit

"Yes, sir. Except . . . there's a lot of luck involved in a penalty shoot-out. Sean Peters sometimes stops a blinder, but he misses easy ones, too. And, if Sean misses one of mine, Kelvin might think he did it on purpose because he's my friend."

"I'm aware of that, Brian," said Mr. Quale. "So we won't have Sean Peters in the net."

"Who will be goalie, sir?"

Mr. Quale raised his eyebrow, inscrutable Evil Warlord-style. "That's the special surprise for tomorrow. Someone who will really test you both. We'll see whether an Ice Man can beat a Show Pony in a penalty shoot-out. Fair enough?"

"Sure, coach."

catastrophe *n.* kuh-taa-stroh-fee. When everything goes totally wrong and you realize your whole life is about to get totally and truly wrecked. (see also "ruin," "disaster," "debacle," "beginning of the end," "complete screw-up").

"WE'VE got plenty of other nice pens," said the sales clerk. She pointed at a selection on the counter. "Why don't you try a Glide-Along, or a Writes-Tuff? And Space Scriptors are very popular with kids these days."

"Can't you check in the back or something?" I said. "I really need an Easyflow pen."

I was desperate now. I had my first session of Special Interest Writing Group that morning. It would probably be a total embarrassment anyway. I'd most likely do my usual useless writing and I'd most likely look like a total idiot in front of everyone, including my Favorite Writer in the Whole World and the Most Desirable Girl in the History of the Galaxy. But maybe, just maybe, if I could get another Easyflow pen, the magic would happen again.

Woolfield Stationers was the third store I'd tried. All the others had said something similar: "We don't stock Easyflow pens anymore." "We haven't seen an Easyflow for years." "Easyflow? Never heard of them."

"Listen," I said to the sales clerk, "I have to get a pink Easyflow pen and I have to get one today!" I thumped my fist into my hand. It felt pretty stupid. "It's absolutely, vitally urgent!"

"Sorry, I'm new here," she said. "My supervisor, Val, has worked in Woolfield since year one. If anyone knows anything about pens, Val does." She called into her microphone, "Val to Checkout Two!"

We waited for Val. I was already going to be late for school. I'd have to think up a creative excuse for missing Mr. Mackington's English class. I could say, um . . . I was so absorbed in writing another fantastic story for Special Interest Writing Group that I didn't notice that three school buses went past without me, and then I had to walk, and on the way I'd stopped to rescue a lady from a savage leopard that had escaped from the zoo. I'd hypnotized the leopard by staring into its yellow eyes until the keepers arrived with the tranquilizer darts. I had no trouble thinking up stuff like that. How come I was so hopeless at writing?

Val arrived.

"This young gentleman is asking about Easyflow pens," said the sales clerk, winking at Val. "He says it's absolutely, vitally urgent." It sounded even worse when she repeated it. Like she wasn't taking me seriously.

But Val was. She looked at me strangely as she asked, "What does a nice young kid like you want an Easyflow for?"

"I just . . . like them," I said lamely.

"I don't think you'll get one these days, love," said Val kindly. "Easyflows didn't last very long. Nice-looking pens, made by a funny little company. Sold like hot cakes at first. Then people started bringing them back . . . with complaints."

"Complaints?" I said.

"There was something peculiar about those Easyflows," said Val, "but no one would say exactly what it was. Woolfields has a money-back, no-questions-asked policy, so we never found out what was going on. It was weird, though."

Weird. Had all Easyflow pens been able to write love stories by themselves? In any case, now nobody would ever find out the truth. The world's last Easyflow pen was crushed into a zillion bits at

Ideas I had TODAY
by BRIAN HOBBLE

Pirates
secretly
love
looking
at them-
selves in
Mirrors!

(* Probably true)

the bottom of Mr. Quale's garbage can.

Val pulled open a drawer under the counter and fumbled in the back of it. "The company that made those Easyflows did make a kids' pen, too," she said. "Youngsters thought they were kind of cute, I remember. You can't buy them anymore, but I just might have one . . . aha, here it is!"

She pulled out another pen and handed it to me. It was pink, and shaped exactly like an Easyflow, but instead of the flowery purple letters on the side, this one had a picture of a magic wand and a trail of silver stars. On the end was a bright red eraser in the shape of a spotted toadstool. It was labeled "Fairy Magic." Val said I could have it for nothing because the toadstool eraser had been used and some of the spots had come off.

The Fairy Magic was the exact opposite of an Easyflow pen. No way was this pen going to write about sweat beading on girls' heaving bosoms. In my hand, it probably wouldn't write anything at all.

As I turned to leave Woolfields, the books caught my eye. Or rather, one particular shelf of books, with the author's name leaping out from a pink card with silver lettering: *Veronica Lovelace*. There were forty-seven of them: *Delilah My Desire* by Veronica Lovelace; *Love Among the Elms* by Veronica Lovelace; *My Pirate My Darling*; *Midnight Kisses*; *Passionate Whispers*. I picked up one called *My Beating Heart* and read the blurb on the back cover. *"Nurse Bethany Brookhampton is in love with handsome heart surgeon Trent Storm. But her own sister Chloe needs an urgent transplant. Both of their fates are in Trent's firm, manly hands."*

I wondered what Veronica Lovelace's writing would be like now that she'd lost her Easyflow pen. She was the lucky one. At least she didn't have to face the Special Interest Writing Group.

It was recess when I sneaked in the school gate. I went straight up to the library to cook up an excuse for my lateness. I'd decided against using the escaped leopard story. To make Mr. Mackington believe it, I'd have to rip my shirt and scratch claw marks on my arm with a compass point—too complicated, too painful. Instead I'd borrow a library book as an alibi. He liked my tadpole story. I could say I'd been doing research for a vitally important science project on the control of cane toads.

I'd just found the section on amphibians when in walked Nathan Lumsdyke. He grabbed me by the elbow and hissed, "Brian, you actually have to return that Easyflow pen right now!" He let go of my elbow and thumped his fist into his hand. "It's absolutely, vitally urgent!"

"Sorry, Nathan," I said. "I lost it."

"Then find it, Brian," he said firmly.

"Nathan, I lost that pen kind of permanently. Kind of very permanently. It's been totally destroyed, actually."

The color drained out of Nathan's face, just like it did out of Spike's face in *A T-Rex Ate My Homework*, when the T-Rex sniffed around his hiding place under Miss Weevil's desk.

"Then I'm actually in extremely serious trouble," he murmured. "Mom nearly had an absolute nervous breakdown last night when she found I'd taken her pen to school. I don't actually know what's so special about them, but she loves those Easyflows. She bought a whole box of them when they first came out, and she's used nothing but Easyflows ever since. The one I gave you was her last one, actually."

What could I do? Nathan had lent me the pen. It did belong to his mom. I had lost it. I didn't have a choice. I had to give up my new pen. I pulled out the Fairy Magic. My hand shook ever so slightly as I handed it to Nathan. "Give her this," I said. "It's made by the same company—exact same shape, exact same color. Rip the toadstool off the end and scratch off the label with a coin. She'll never notice the difference."

Nathan let out his breath in a long sigh of relief, just like Spike did when the T-Rex ate Miss Weevil instead of him. "Okay," he said.

He tucked the Fairy Magic pen into his breast

pocket. As it joined seventeen other pens of different shapes and colors, I felt like Spike, watching his last remaining friend (the nerdy but loyal Errol Pong) grow fangs, scales, and claws and join the herd of dinosaurs destroying the school. Like Spike, my last faint chance dissolved into thin air and I could no longer clutch at forlorn shreds of hope.

Nathan, on the other hand, was much cheerier now. "This Special Interest Writing Group . . ." he said. "I've actually got an excellent idea for a descriptive story, all set in our backyard. What are you going to write about, Brian?"

"Nothing," I said. This was absolutely true, of course.

"Why not?" asked Nathan.

My brain fumbled around in its back shed, looking for a brilliant excuse to explain why I was going to stop writing forever. My mouth came up with one. "Because I've been bitten by a mosquito, Nathan."

"A mosquito, Brian?"

"It's infected me with a rare form of periocerebralitis," said my mouth.

"Perio-sebby-what?"

There was no stopping my mouth now. "It's a brain disease," it rattled on. "The doctors say I'll stay a beautiful person, red-hot babe magnet, soccer star, and all that. But tragically the virus has attacked the creative part of my brain." I pressed my hand to the left side of my forehead, and for good measure added a brave little smile.

"Really?" said Nathan. He was swallowing that story pretty well, thought my brain. If Nathan believed me, I could refine my excuse into something truly brilliant and use it on more important people: Mr. Mackington, Lancelot Cummins, Cassandra . . .

"The doctors tell me I may never again write a

creative story," I continued, sighing to show Nathan how sad this made me feel.

Nathan pulled his glasses down to the tip of his nose and peered at me across the rims. "That actually sounds like bull," he said, poking the glasses up into position again.

Okay, so I'd have to think up a better excuse than the brain disease one, but I wasn't going to that writing class. No way.

I went to the counter to check out my alibi book, *101 Interesting Uses for a Dead Toad*.

"Ahem . . . could I have a word with you . . . er . . . ?" said Lancelot Cummins.

LANCELOT Cummins led me into Ms. Kitto's little glass cubicle behind the library counter. I wondered how Ms. Kitto was enjoying sharing a small office with someone who wrote books with lots of butts in them. She was over by the computers, telling off some senior boys she'd caught playing DeathTrap when they should have been researching modern history.

Lancelot Cummins pulled out a seat for me and pushed aside a stack of the little kids' stories. During the week he'd been doing story-writing workshops with all the classes in the school. First graders had been writing the adventures of a character called Honey the Funny Bunny.

"Brian Hobble, isn't it?"

"That's right, sir."

"Oh please, call me Lance. After all, Brian, you're a fellow writer."

"Am I?" I couldn't believe this. The author of really cool, fantastic books like *A T-Rex Ate My Homework* was calling me a "fellow writer"! Lancelot Cummins shuffled pink bunny pictures around on the table.

"You've written some very special stories this week, Brian."

"Um, yes, Mr., er . . . "

"You obviously love writing, Brian."

"It's all right, I suppose."

The great Lancelot Cummins was talking to me! This should have been one of the most exciting moments of my life. Instead it was one of the most embarrassing.

"I'd like to see more of your work, Brian. I read a lot of young people's writing, much of it good, but yours really is quite . . . extraordinary."

You're telling me it's extraordinary, I thought. No young person in the history of the world had ever written anything as extraordinary as the stories I'd written in the last two days. Should I tell him that I hadn't really written the stories myself? But I had written them, sort of.

And now he wouldn't shut up about it . . .

"I loved your frog story, Brian," he said. "The idea of two tadpoles in love is fresh and brave and original. It was funny and moving at the same time. It was even, well . . . dare I say it . . . it was quite sexy!"

This was getting worse and worse.

"You found a brilliant metaphor for the way people change and grow. And a powerful argument against humans exploiting helpless creatures in the name of scientific research. Mr. Mackington tells me you wrote the whole thing in less than half an hour!"

"Er, yes, I suppose I must have, sir."

"It reads like a story that you just couldn't stop yourself from writing, Brian. It leaps from the page as if it had written itself."

"Er, yes, Mr. Cummins." How did he know? That was exactly what had happened.

"If I could offer just a little advice though . . . " he said.

"Sure, Mr. Cummins."

"Next time, Brian, I'd like to see you write something more from your own personal experience."

"My personal experience?"

"Your first story, about the mailman and the housewife . . . um . . . ?"

"Arabella?"

"Yes, that story was really clever and you were very brave to write it, and read it aloud in class. I suppose your friends may have teased you a little afterward."

"Yes, they did a bit."

"And the tadpole story—brilliant! But Brian, you're writing love stories, and boys your age don't have much experience with love. Do you?"

"I suppose not." (Not if you don't count being totally crazy about Cassandra Wyman.)

"The love scenes in the story didn't seem to quite come from you, Brian. They sounded like the writing of an older writer, with more life experience."

"Really?" (Such as Veronica Lovelace maybe?)

"Don't take this the wrong way, Brian. It's a great achievement to mimic the style of romantic fiction the way you did. Now I'd love to see you write a story more about yourself, your life, and the things you understand. That's what I'd like you to try in Special Interest Writing Group."

"Um, sure, Mr. Cummins."

"You are a great talent, Brian. I'm jealous. I wish writing would flow out of my pen like it flows out of yours."

"But you've written heaps of books, Mr. Cummins!"

"It's never easy for me, Brian. Most of the things I write are so bad I wouldn't dare show them to anybody. I write ten stories for every one that's good enough to go into a book. The last few years I've found it impossible to write stories I'm happy with. Do you know I haven't published anything since *The Haunted Dunny Brush*?"

"I read it, Mr., er, Cummins. It was really good."

"It's nice of you to say so, Brian, but I wrote it

over three years ago. Since then, nothing's working. I sit at the desk every morning, but I can't write for five minutes without getting stuck. My publishers are nagging me about new books but, to be honest, I'm a bit tired of writing books about snot and butts and monsters."

"Why don't you write about something else then?" I asked.

"I want to . . . very much. I want to write something serious, with meaning and feeling. But when I try it just seems, well, too hard. Have you heard of writer's block?" Of course I had. My whole life was one big writer's block. Until I got that Easyflow pen I'd never been able to write three lines without hitting a writer's block the size of Mount Everest.

"That's why I've turned to teaching," he said. "I think to myself, Lance, even if you can't write any more yourself, maybe you can help someone else to do it better. The trouble is, I'm not much of a teacher either. Boys and girls enjoy my books, but they find me dry and boring when they meet me in person. I know most of them think my classes are a bit serious and intellectual. I've got weird stories inside me somewhere, but in real life I can't help being . . . ordinary."

I felt a bit sorry for him. Lancelot Cummins

was so successful, but here he was telling a schoolkid how disappointed he was in himself. Maybe that was a bad thing about being a writer. No matter how well you did it, you always wished you could do better.

Lancelot Cummins went on. "I envy you, Brian. Most boys your age are only interested in soccer and girls. You're lucky to be an unusual boy who loves writing, and who attacks it with such commitment and humor and daring. It's so important to me to encourage a star pupil like you. It makes the work I'm trying to do all seem worthwhile."

I shifted nervously in my seat. "Er . . . Mr. Cummins . . . I don't think you're a bad teacher. I've learned heaps about writing this week." Which was sort of half true, after all.

"Brian, you have a rare gift! I want to use your work as an inspiration to others in the Special Interest Writing Group."

I had to put a stop to this before it got really embarrassing. There was only one way to do it. I had to tell him the truth, the whole truth, and nothing but the truth.

"Look, Mr. Cummins," I said, "there's been this really big mistake. I'm really a hopeless writer. I don't have any talent myself. It's just this pen I was using . . ."

"What pen?"

I needed a little puff on my asthma inhaler before I could go on. Deep breath in, deep breath out. "You see, I got this pink Easyflow pen . . . "

I told him everything, from beginning to end. About how I borrowed the pen from Nathan, and how I was really embarrassed about writing the love stories. I told him about the fight over the soccer penalty. I told him about thinking Mr. Quale had been fired, the embarrassing meeting with Mrs. Davenport, and how Mr. Moray took over as coach. I told him how I lent the pen to Mr. Moray, and what happened when he used it, and how he smashed it and how I'd never be able to get another one. "So you see," I finished, "without that Easyflow pen, I can't write at all."

Lancelot Cummins leaned back in his seat. "Incredible, Brian!"

"I really shouldn't be in Special Interest Writing Group."

He shook his head. "What an extraordinary imagination you have, Brian Hobble!" he said. "I could never have thought up anything like that."

He thought I'd made the story up! I suppose I couldn't blame him. The whole incident with the Easyflow pen was so weird that nobody would believe it. There was no point in me telling anyone else about it, insisting that it had really happened. If I did that, everyone would think I had a screw loose. I had to pretend I'd invented the story.

"You can use my Easyflow pen idea in your next book, if it helps," I said. "I think you could write it really well."

"It wouldn't be fair for me to take an idea like that from a fellow writer, Brian. That's your story, and you have to be the one to write it down. I know you can do it."

Nathan Lumsdyke was tapping on the glass. "Excuse me, Mr. Cummins, but actually the Special Interest Writing Group is waiting for you in Room ninteen. We've been there quite a while, actually."

Lancelot Cummins put his hand on my shoulder as we left the library. He was about to have another great disappointment. What would he think when he saw that without that Easyflow pen his star writing pupil couldn't write a thing?

"Come on, Brian," said Lancelot Cummins. "Let's show these other writers a thing or two."

"Er, sure . . . Lance."

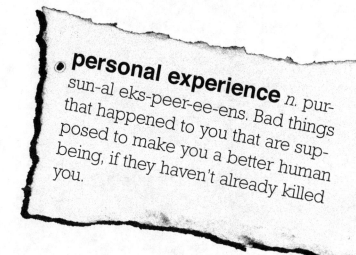

personal experience *n.* pur-sun-al eks-peer-ee-ens. Bad things that happened to you that are supposed to make you a better human being, if they haven't already killed you.

MOST of the Special Interest Writing Group were senior students. Robert Fotin and Jessica Grey, the editors of the *Garunga School Gazette*, were lounging on desks at the back of the room, talking to Abby Post's big sister, Brittany. Of the others, there were some faces I recognized, but I didn't really know them.

The seniors in our school were like superior beings whom we never dared to talk to, and they sure wouldn't know me. Cassandra, Nathan, and I were the youngest there. Of course the seniors normally regarded little kids like us as beneath their interest. They barely glanced in our direction as Nathan and I came in, but I saw Brittany nudge Robert Fotin and whisper something. He looked at me and laughed.

Cool things
to say to a girl
when she says
she likes you!!!

© By B. HOBBLE

① —THANKS

② Yeah... I know I'm cool.

③ You're not bad either.

Miserably, I took a seat next to Cassandra. It was strange to feel miserable sitting next to Cassandra Wyman. Only a couple of days ago I would have given anything to sit next to her, but this was going to be the worst, most embarrassing hour of my entire life.

174

I wished something would happen to stop that awful class. I prayed for a fire alarm, or an earthquake, or a flash flood, or a lightning strike. It would even have been good if a T-Rex stuck its claws in through the window and plucked me out of there. On second thought, it would be better if the T-Rex plucked Nathan Lumsdyke out of there. He was sliding into a seat on the other side of Cassandra.

Was it just my imagination, or did she shift a little away from Nathan . . . toward me? I caught a whiff of a clean, lemony soapy smell as she flicked her blond ponytail. I felt the warmth of her shoulder as it pressed against my shirt sleeve. She wasn't looking at me. She was giving all her attention to Lancelot Cummins as he started the class.

"Welcome, writers," he said. "I've had the pleasure over the last couple of days of reading a little of your work, and I have to say how impressed I am by your efforts. Congratulations.

"You've written about a wide range of subjects, but what I'd like to see now is a quick piece of personal writing to let us know who you are."

Lancelot Cummins wrote in big letters on the whiteboard:

WRITE WHAT YOU KNOW

"What I'd like each of you to try," said

Lancelot Cummins, "is to write about something from your personal experience. Perhaps you know a lot about horses, or motorcycles, or even just about the people in your family.

"When I was a kid I was interested in insects and my sister had a collection of Barbie dolls. So in *Ants in My Pants* I imagined what it would be like if a column of soldier ants carried off Ken, and Action Barbie had to rescue him. I knew a bit about ants and I knew far too much about Barbies, so I could write about them quite well.

"If you know all about your subject, you'll find you have lots more to say about it. If you write honestly, describing little details, then your writing will be interesting to others. So pick something you know lots about and tell us about it. Go!"

Heads went down. Nathan was writing. Cassandra was writing. I groped in the depths of my backpack and pulled out a scruffy green pen. I opened my notebook. I looked around the room. Everybody was writing—except for me. I couldn't think of a single thing to write about.

I caught Lancelot Cummins's eye. He winked at me as if to say, "Go on, Brian, write something brilliant to inspire these other kids." Lancelot Cummins expected me to be a writing genius.

Cassandra paused from her writing for a

moment to look at me. She glanced down at my empty page. She smiled that smile. She expected me to write something brilliant, too.

I put my pen in my mouth and pretended to be considering what to write. I pretended I wouldn't be satisfied with just putting down any old story and handing it in. I tried to look as though I was thinking hard, planning a piece of writing that would be really clever and different and original. Except that my mind was a total blank.

I chewed the end of the green pen. Yuck! Shocking taste. Where had it been? I looked at the pen. No markings. Nothing special about it— just a green pen. I couldn't even remember where I'd gotten it. It was just one of those ordinary, nothing sort of pens that magically appear in your bag from time to time. Maybe they breed in there. I wiped the pen on my sleeve. I didn't belong here. I had no special interest in writing. Take away my Easyflow pen and I was immediately back to the old unimaginative Brian Hobble. In a few minutes, everyone was going to find out just how hopeless I really was.

I stared at the whiteboard:

WRITE WHAT YOU KNOW

What did I know about? Nothing. Nothing

interesting: school, Garunga, my house, TV shows, Macho Burgers, bands, soccer . . . Soccer. I wasn't a great player, but I did know something about the game.

"Write honestly," Lancelot Cummins said. "Describe little details."

I looked at the ordinary, average, no-name green pen. Then suddenly I remembered where it had come from. And whom it belonged to. I'd accidentally brought it with me after Vince and I wrote down our lists of colorful expressions—in Mrs. Davenport's office.

I touched the pen to the paper . . .

"You couldn't kick a goal if it knelt down in front of you with its butt in the air!" "You couldn't kick over an empty bucket, buddy." "Where'd you get those legs you're wearing, sonny? He pulled 'em off a stick insect!"

Eastburn Eagles players swarm around the boy, like a pack of hyenas around a wounded baby antelope on a wildlife show. On the sidelines, the Garunga Glory fans are going crazier than a TV studio audience when someone's playing for a million dollars. If their

> hero gets this penalty they'll win the
> district final!

The more I wrote, the more I found I could imagine it all. It was like I was watching next Friday's game.

> "That skinny little kid's your penalty
> kicker?" the ref asks Vince (Speedy)
> Peretti, the handsome Garunga captain.
> Even the ref thinks there must be some
> mistake. Vince turns to his team, lined up
> behind him. The incredible bulk of the
> powerful Arthur Neerlander. The sneering
> Kelvin Moray, jealous it's not him taking the
> penalty, but hoping all the same that
> the kid might win them the game.
> Tangles, Mad Cow, Seven Eleven . . . Vince
> looks back toward the pale, serious,
> intelligent-looking boy, calmly pulling up his
> socks in the penalty area. "We call him
> the Ice Man," he says.

179

I could see it all happening in front of me, just like I was standing on the sidelines. Like I was there, standing between Mr. Quale and Mrs. Davenport.

The Eastburn Eagles grin and whisper to each other. This puny little Garunga kid is no match for their goalie. Their goalie is their star player, a huge German called Klaus Beckenbauer, otherwise known as The Berlin Wall. He hasn't let a goal through all season. He's saved fifteen penalties with awesome diving saves. The Ice Man isn't fazed. His face is as expressionless as a killer zombie's. He's cooler than a nudist at the North Pole. He's cooler than a frozen TV dinner before your mom microwaves it. The ref places the ball on the penalty spot. The Ice Man stands still. Only his lips move a little. He's whistling to himself! The tune is "I Did It My Way"! He doesn't look even a bit nervous. The crowd goes silent in amazement. That Ice Man kid is so cool!

All I had to do was write down what I was seeing in my mind—it was easy. Just like what I used to do when I was little, conducting a running commentary as I played whole games on my own, kicking a ball around the backyard.

> The Ice Man goes quiet. Beckenbauer is
> ready. The ref nods to them both. He
> blows his whistle. The Ice Man takes
> three quick steps . . .

Hey! The power I had! I could make anything happen. It wasn't great writing maybe, but I was totally grabbed by it. Boy, was it fun! It was nothing like the mushy, slushy Veronica Lovelace stuff. This was coming from me, with my sort of language, and sometimes my colorful expressions were as good as Mr. Quale's. I was in control. I could do whatever I liked!

> . . . His cleat is a blur. A clean whack,
> leather on leather! The Berlin Wall dives,
> but he's never had to stop a kick like this

one. The ball hits him flush on the chest. Its force slams him into the goalpost. The ball goes on, ripping its way through the netting like a bullet shot through wet toilet paper. Who would believe that the little Ice Man kid would have that much power in those thin legs? The ref's whistle! Goal! The cheers! Garunga are District Champions!!! The crowd floods onto the field. The Ice Man raises his left eyebrow and allows himself the smallest of smiles, like an evil warlord whose army has just smashed through the gates and conquered the city.

I chuckled when I wrote it, I cackled to myself as I read it over and changed a few things, and, best of all, when I volunteered to read it aloud to the Special Interest Writing Group, even the senior kids laughed at the funny bits. So did Cassandra Wyman! When I'd finished reading it, Lancelot Cummins gave me a big thumbs-up. I hadn't let him down.

After the class, all the other kids clustered around to shake my hand and pat me on the back.

Jessica Grey said she'd publish my story in the *Gazette*. When I showed it to Vince at lunchtime, he asked me to read parts of the story over and over, especially the bit about him being handsome. Abby's sister, Brittany, had told her how good my soccer story was, and after school Abby and Sarah and Sofie got me to sign their notebooks, just in case I ever became a famous author. They drew little pink hearts around my signature. I felt really proud of myself. Even prouder than when I got the real penalty in the real game. I was a writer!

As I was waiting for the bus, Cassandra Wyman came up to me. While I'd been writing the story she'd been sitting right beside me but, the funny thing was, I hadn't noticed her at all. I'd been so into the story, so totally on Planet Soccer.

"It was a great story, Brian," said Cassandra. "It even got me interested in soccer."

"I thought you weren't a very sporty person?"

She smiled. "Ask me again after I see the game on Friday."

"Really, Cassandra?"

"I'll be there. I might even cheer if the Ice Man scores a goal."

It was nice to get this sort of attention—especially from Cassandra.

"I don't know if I'll score any goals in the final," I said. "I'm not really such a great player. I just kind of lucked out last time."

I told her about the problem I'd had with Kelvin Moray and how Mr. Quale was giving us a penalty shoot-out tomorrow afternoon. For me, the penalty shoot-out with Kelvin would be even more exciting than the game itself.

"Sounds like something I shouldn't miss," said Cassandra. There was that smile again. "Can I come and watch?"

"Sure, if you want to."

"Good. I can be one of those sick, obsessed sports fans who turn up to watch team practices."

There was something else I wanted to ask her.

"Cassandra?"

"Yes, Brian?"

"I know you like writing and all that, but, well, what do you write about?"

She shrugged. "I don't know, just ordinary things."

"Like, what did you do for that 'Write What You Know' lesson?"

"Oh, nothing anyone else would find interesting."

"Can I have a look at it, Cassandra?" I'd never seen any of the stories she'd written. That's what you got for being quiet in class. I didn't have the faintest idea what sort of stories a girl like her would write.

She pulled her notebook from her bag and thrust it out at me. "It's not a really exciting story like yours, Brian. I'm not much good at jokes and stuff like that. It's just a bit about my family."

The story was pretty short. Most of it was crossed out and rewritten. She hadn't been sure whether she wanted to write it or not, and it had been really hard to get it right.

Stevie. People say he's got problems, but he's always laughing. Sometimes little kids point at him in the street, and sometimes he points back at them. They say he will never have a normal life. They say he will never learn to take care of himself. They say he will never grow up. We should be sad about that. But when I come back from school, light shines from Stevie's face. He runs to the door. "Cassie home! Cassie home!" Stevie will always be a child. Stevie will always be my brother. Stevie and Cassie will always love each other.

Wow! I didn't know anything at all about Cassandra Wyman. But I wanted to know more, much more. And I wanted to read more of her writing. "This is fantastic . . . Cassie," I said.

"Is it all right?" she asked, "I didn't know what else to write about."

"It's so simple, but it makes you feel . . . I could never write like this."

"You don't need to, Brian. You can't write like I

write. I can't write the way you do. Everybody writes in their own special way. It's like your signature. Or your voice."

This was amazing! I was having a serious discussion about writing . . . with a girl . . . with Cassandra Wyman! Cassie.

One person who hadn't congratulated me on my story was Nathan Lumsdyke. The next morning he sidled up to me on the way to school, with a puzzled look on his face.

"What's wrong with you, Nathan?" I asked.

Without a word he handed me a notebook marked *Special Interest Writing—author Nathan Lumsdyke.*

Nathan skipped and tripped down through the sweet peas to the bottom of the pretty garden. Mr. Sun was shining so gaily and bees buzzed cheerily in the blossom trees.

"Hee, hee, hee!" giggled Twinkle Toes, the jolly little pixie. "We're going to have such merry fun today, Nathan, making daisy chains for the friendly bluebirds!"

"Oh goody goody gumdrops," laughed Nathan, jumping up and down and clapping his chubby little hands together, "and Mommy says I'm allowed to go on a butterfly ride with you, all the way to Tinkly Town Hollow. Just so long as I'm back by dinner time . . ."

There were eight pages of this stuff!

Nathan whispered, "I didn't mean to write that, Brian. It sort of just . . . came out." He took off his glasses and breathed on the lenses, then polished them furiously on the corner of his shirt. I noticed what was peeping out of his breast pocket—the spotted toadstool eraser from the Fairy Magic pen.

"I thought, Brian, you might . . . be able to tell me why it happened, actually," he said. (Lie detector starts blinking quietly.)

What could I say to him?

"Actually, Nathan, I don't have a clue." (Lie detector flat as a dead person's monitor on life support.)

I couldn't wait to read the next Veronica Lovelace book. It was sure to be very interesting!

farewell n & v.i. fair-wel.
Good-bye, see you later, maybe
we might keep in touch for a
while but we probably won't, so
have a nice life anyway.

"GOOD luck, Brian," said Lancelot Cummins. "You will keep on writing, won't you?"

It was his last day at the school. On the title page of my tattered copy of *Escape from Planet Zog*, he'd written:

> To Brian,
> With admiration for a fellow writer!
> Lancelot Cummins

He shook my hand and gave me a card. "Brian, this is my e-mail address. Don't spread it around the whole school, if you don't mind, and don't give it to that Nathan Lumsdyke guy. But if you ever want to show me anything you've written, I promise I won't be critical. I'd just really like to read it."

"Thanks, sir," I said.

"I've been thinking a lot about your Easyflow pen story, Brian."

"So have I," I said.

"It's something you ought to write down."

"You can use it if you want to, Mr. Cummins," I said. "I mean, you're a real writer. You said you needed good ideas."

"A writer always needs good ideas, Brian. But that Easyflow pen one, that's yours. Write it. Please."

It sounded easy, but I still wasn't sure. "What if I can't make it good enough?"

"Good enough for what? It's a great idea, Brian, so just do it. Go!"

I went.

Over the next few weeks I e-mailed him some ideas for stories. *"There's this blood-sucking vampire, and he meets this kid called Kelvin who thinks he's fantastic . . ."* *"There's this boy who likes a girl, but she doesn't like soccer and he does . . ."*

Each time he e-mailed back he asked what was happening with my Easyflow pen story. So in the end I wrote it. It wasn't easy. It took me quite a while, but it was fun. Now you've just read it. *Weird stuff*, wasn't it?

oops! *excl.* oops. Oops, whoops, oh dear, silly me, you total idiot!

SORRY, I nearly forgot . . . the soccer final! You've probably noticed that this book is nearly over and I haven't told you anything about the game of the century: the district final.

You want to know who won. I'm not sure I'm going to tell you. I'm the writer, you see. I can leave you wanting more. I can stop anytime I like. I can leave you with the hero hanging by his fingernails over a cage of hungry crocodiles. I can make you wait, forever if I want to—or maybe until the next book. I have the power.

Are you disappointed?

Okay then, I'll tell you about the penalty shootout with Kelvin Moray instead. That was exciting enough, because of Mr. Quale's big surprise.

We'll finish with that . . .

self-belief *n.* self buh-leef.
When you feel that, whatever
happens, everything's going to
be okay in the end.

PRESSURE: the penalty shoot-out between me
and Kelvin Moray.

Best of ten shots, with the winner to take the
penalty if we get one in tomorrow's final.

Mr. Quale tosses a coin to see who goes first. I
call "Heads." Heads it is. "I'll go first," I say.

The whole team is watching me. Vince, Arthur,
Rocco, Sean Peters. Mr. Quale is watching. Kelvin
Moray is watching. It will be his turn next. And
this time, Cassie Wyman is watching me as well.

A big black man with frizzy gray hair spins the
ball in his hands and places it on the penalty spot.
He's Roberto Santos, legendary Brazilian soccer
coach. He's one half of Mr. Quale's special surprise. The other half of the surprise is on the goal
line. Juan Pieros, goalie for Brazil's under-twenty-
one National side. Mr. Quale met Roberto and
Juan at the Coaching Clinic and invited them to
our final practice.

Juan's just spent half an hour working with Sean Peters and giving him some pointers on guarding the goal. All our players have tried kicking goals with Juan in the net. Not many made it through. Now I have to put a penalty past him. Juan Pieros is dark, tall, gangly, supple . . . and very focused. He won't want any schoolkid to score against him, not with Roberto Santos watching.

Juan Pieros doesn't speak English. It was hilarious watching him mime what was wrong with Sean Peters's guarding. He can't talk to us, but he grins as he shakes hands with me and Kelvin Moray. The alien renovators are at work in my chest again: *Chugga-chugga-chugga!*

I won't use the asthma inhaler this time. It stays in my pocket until this is over. I'm not giving Kelvin Moray any excuse to say my performance was enhanced.

Deep breath in, deep breath out.

Maybe Juan Pieros will stop my penalty shot, and maybe he won't. Maybe Kelvin Moray will beat me in this shoot-out and maybe he won't. Maybe if I win, Cassie Wyman will be impressed. Maybe if I lose, she'll like me even more, because she's not a very sporty person and everybody loves an underdog. There's still a final to play tomorrow. There'll be another soccer competition next year.

Lots more games. Then plenty more tests coming up. I'll pass some and I'll fail some. I'm cool with that.

Ice Man, you can do this thing! Brian Hobble, believe in yourself. Believe! Believe, Brian Hobble, don't be a septic. (That word still doesn't sound right—I must check it. Not now, though. I'm too busy.)

Mr. Quale blows his whistle. Go! I'm Brian The Ice Man Hobble—soccer superstar, wonder writer, red-hot babe magnet!

Three quick steps and . . .

The End

Dreams
—
August 6

An Albatros.
flies in
circles
trying to
catch
its
tail.

*Note: Must look up symbols book —
see what Albatross in dreams means...
Probably symbol of getting rich!!